ONE NIGHT
WITH
THE Billionaire

ROSE M. COOPER

OSHUN
PUBLICATIONS
oshunpublications.com

One Night with the Billionaire © Copyright 2021 by Rose M. Cooper

Published by Oshun Publications
9 Old Kings Road STE. 123-1038
Palm Coast, FL 32137
www.oshunpublications.com

Disclaimer
This is a work of fiction. Names, characters, places, and incidents either are the product of the author's imagination or are used fictitiously. Any resemblance to actual persons, living or dead, events, or locales is entirely coincidental.

Book design by oliviaprodesign
www.fiverr.com/oliviaprodesign

ISBN 978-1-950378-67-8 (Paperback)
ISBN 978-1-956319-21-7 (Hardback)
ISBN 978-1-950378-66-1 (eBook)

Also by Rose M. Cooper

THERE ARE ALSO AUDIOBOOKS!

rosemaecooper.com/audiobooks

GET YOUR GENRE FIX TODAY! JOIN MY NEWSLETTER FOR MY RECOMMENDATIONS AND UPDATES!

ROSEMAECOOPER.COM

CHAPTER 1
A Little Mishap

Kiana had another few minutes left on the treadmill when her phone strapped to her arm beeped. She glanced down to see the picture of her best friend, Magda, blinking up at her. Careful not to lose her stride, Kiana hit the answer button.

"Hey," Kiana breathed as she adjusted the earphone cord.

"Hi there, stranger," Magda's cheerful voice purred through the headphones. "I was wondering if we are still on for our brunch on Saturday."

"Of course," Kiana grinned. "I look forward to our Saturday liquid brunches."

"I think after last Saturday, we should try to get a little more food this time," Magda laughed. "I did not like the morning after feeling from too many mimosas."

"Yes, but think of all the fun we had." Kiana's grin widened. "I did not realize just how well you could sing Whitney Houston songs."

"Oh, please don't remind me," Magda begged. "We can never return to that karaoke bar again, ever!"

"Why?" Kiana teased. "You won two prizes and a trophy!"

"Okay, I am going to hang up now," Magda warned her. "My cheeks are flaming still from my debut as a singer."

"Okay, okay," Kiana placated Magda. "I will say no more on the subject."

"Where are you?" Magda asked. "You sound out of breath, and it is rather loud."

"I am at the gym, where I am every day at this time," Kiana informed Magda.

"Right," Magda said. "I did not realize it was that time already. It has been such a hectic day at the boutique."

"That's a good thing, though, right?" Kiana adjusted the speed on the treadmill to a walk for her cool down. "It means your business is booming."

"I would not say booming," Magda corrected Kiana. "I would say doing extremely well."

"I hope you still have that shirt I asked you to put aside?" Kiana asked. "I will get it when I get paid next week."

"Yes," Magda assured Kiana. "It is still here waiting for you. I must go. I will call you later."

"Sure," Kiana moved her neck from side to side as she started to cool down. "Chat later." The call ended.

Kiana slowed the treadmill down a little more while doing a few deep breathing exercises before making it stop. She stood on the equipment, stretching her muscles before grabbing her towel and water to head for the locker rooms.

As Kiana rounded the corner to the locker room, her foot skidded on a puddle of water. As she tried to steady herself, her other foot slipped out, and she landed with a thud on the cold hard floor.

The back of Kiana's head connected with the tiles on the floor; as it did, it sent shockwaves of pain coursing through her entire body. Kiana felt like she was vibrating with pain as black dots floated around her eyes. She gasped for breath, having been winded by the impact of her fall. The roaring in her ears blocked out all the sounds around her.

Kiana did not know how long she had been on the floor. Time seemed to have stood still while she lay there, unable to move. When the dots cleared from her vision, a pair of strong whiskey-brown eyes stared down at her. Kiana blinked, a little confused; when she opened her eyes, the man staring down at her came into focus. She blinked again, but his handsome face was still there when her eyes opened.

Kiana could see the man's face and lips moving, but his voice sounded like he was so far away; she could hardly hear him. She shut her eyes tightly, taking in a few deep breaths. The sounds around her started to filter back into her ears as she willed her body to relax.

"Miss?" the man with stunning brown eyes called to her with concern. "Can you hear me?"

Kiana tried to speak but could not find her voice, so she nodded.

"That was quite the fall you had," the man said. "Can I help you up?"

Kiana nodded again. She managed to raise her arm towards him, but instead, he bent down and scooped her up as if she weighed nothing more than a pillow. Right now, Kiana felt like a downy pillow with feathers fluttering in her stomach being held in the man's powerful arms.

"You can bring her this way, sir," the gym manager rushed over to them. "I am so sorry about this."

"You should be," the man's deep voice rumbled through his solid chest, pressed tightly against Kiana's arm. "That spill was reported to your staff more than ten minutes ago. That pool of water should have been taken care of right away!"

"Of course, you are right, sir," the manager said apologetically. "We are a little short-staffed today due to the bad weather, and that leak has only just appeared."

"There you go," the man put Kiana down gently on the bed in the gym's infirmary. "My friend, Hayden, is a doctor; I asked one of the gym's staff to get him."

"That won't be necessary," Kiana swallowed; her throat felt dry, and her head was starting to throb. "I am sure I am ..." She tried to sit up, but the world swayed.

"No," the man shook his head and gently pushed her back on the bed. "I don't think you should be doing that. Wait for Hayden; I promise you he does not bite." The man grinned, adding a boyish charm to his devilishly handsome face.

"Well, that remains to be seen," a deep voice turned their heads towards the door.

"Hi, Hayden," the blue-eyed man greeted the tall, well-built man who stepped up to the bed.

"Thank you so much for taking time out of your training, Dr. Baxter," the manager said nervously. "Of course, we will pay for Miss Bridges' consultation and treatment."

"I am sure you will," Hayden popped his doctor's bag onto the counter next to Kiana. "Hi, I'm Hayden Baxter." He smiled at Kiana while cleaning his hands and getting ready to examine her. "Can you tell me your name?"

"Kiana," Kiana said hoarsely. Her head was pounding now. "Kiana Bridges."

Hayden looked at the manager, who nodded his head in confirmation.

"Well, that is a good start," Hayden smiled warmly at her. "How do you know Ronan here?" He took out a small flashlight.

"We don't know each other," Ronan informed Hayden. "I rushed to try and grab Miss Bridges when she slipped, but I was not quick enough."

"I was asking Miss Bridges," Hayden admonished Ronan. "Do you mind if I give you a quick examination?"

"No," Kiana shook her head.

"Okay, you two, I need you to leave the room, please," Hayden, who towered over both the men in the room, gave them a tight smile.

"I will be right outside the door," Ronan assured Kiana. "Oh, by the way, I'm Ronan." He gave Kiana a sexy smile.

"Kiana," Kiana managed a weak smile back.

Under other circumstances, she would have flirted back, but she was sure she was about to …

Before she could stop herself, she sat up and vomited all over Ronan.

"Oh my word, Kiana," Magda helped Kiana onto the sofa. "That is a massive lump on the back of your head."

"It aches like crazy," Kiana let Magda fuss over her. "I feel like a cartoon character with a mountain of a bump protruding from my skull."

"Don't be silly," Magda laughed at Kiana's description of her lump. "You cannot see it with that thick dark hair of yours."

"Just as well, I did not go for that short haircut last week," Kiana's eyes wanted to close; she felt so sleepy. "Those pain meds are making me so drowsy."

"I will go get you a glass of water," Magda told Kiana. "You get some sleep. I will be right here when you wake up." She held up the latest novel she was reading. "That gorgeous new doctor of yours told me not to let you out of my sight for the next few days."

"Please, let's not talk about Dr. Baxter," Kiana's cheeks become colored and not from pain. "I just hope I never have to see his friend again."

"You mean the one you emptied the contents of your

stomach onto?" Magda laughed as Kiana's cheeks burned up. "Sorry, but that beats my karaoke night, hands down."

"How are you going to go to work?" Kiana's eyes started to droop as she changed the subject. She was still mortified that she had thrown upon the man who had saved her from the floor.

"Chloe and I can take turns looking after the store," Magda shrugged. "I am sure she will love getting paid to be out of the store for a couple of hours. It is only for the next two days while you are recovering."

"Thanks, Magda," Kiana smiled gratefully at her friend before her eyes closed, and she drifted off into a fitful sleep with dreams filled with images of heart-stopping brown eyes.

CHAPTER 2
When One Door Closes...

"Of course, I am going to go out with Magda tomorrow," Kiana snarled. "I am feeling a lot better, and Dr. Baxter said my recovery was going well."

"Who is this, Dr. Baxter, anyway?" Owen asked Kiana. "I thought Dr. Thompson was your doctor?"

"She is," Kiana told Owen as calmly as she could. "Dr. Baxter is the doctor who saw me when I had the accident at the gym."

Owen was starting to try Kiana's patience. She could not remember the last time he had stayed the night, let alone the last time they had gone on a date. He was always too busy with some case or the other. Kiana was surprised that Owen had taken a few minutes from his busy Friday night to pop around with Chinese food. Owen had some big court case he needed to prepare for. They were supposed to have gone out to Kiana's favorite restaurant for dinner. Still, Owen decided it would be better for them to stay home.

"I don't like the idea of you going out when you are not well," Owen told her.

"I am fine," Kiana said exasperatedly. "You do this nearly every Friday when you know it is my Saturday brunch day with Magda."

"I do not!" Owen said indignantly. "I am concerned about what a bad influence Magda is over you, though." He dug into his noodles. "Last time I heard, the two of you went to some Karaoke bar."

"I still want to know who told you that," Kiana slammed her food box on the coffee table. "I do not appreciate being spied on, Owen."

"I was not spying on you," Owen's cheek had heated up. "A friend merely saw the two of you going into that dive bar and thought to follow you out of concern."

"Concern for whom, Owen?" Kiana folded her arms over her chest. She was curled up with her bare feet on the sofa. "If it is who I think it is, I am pretty sure she was more concerned for you."

"If you are talking about Renee," Owen's eyes searched Kiana's. "You know that there is nothing between us. I explained that relationship to you."

"Yes," Kiana sighed. "You and she had booty calls." She rolled her eyes. "You are such an idiot if you do not know that your booty calls meant much more to her than you thought."

"We work together," Owen said patiently. "You know how I feel about dating from the working pool."

"But random nights of passion with someone you work with is okay?" Kiana sneered.

"That was a long time ago," Owen raised his eyebrows, and his voice dipped like he was speaking to a naughty child. "I had just started at the DA's office. I didn't know better, and neither did Renee. We were both just having fun."

"Whatever," Kiana waved her hands before jumping off the sofa to go to the kitchen. "Do you want a glass of wine?"

"Should you be drinking?" Owen looked back at her.

"It's been four days since my concussion," Kiana hissed. "I'm not pregnant!"

"Yes, please," Owen's cheeks warmed again. Talking about pregnancy and anything that skirted the borders of that type of commitment made him panic.

"There you go," Kiana put the glass on the table in front of Owen. "Are you staying over tonight?" She gave him a sultry smile.

It had been a few weeks since they had been intimate. Kiana needed a distraction to get a pair of soft brown eyes infused with green, connected to a sexy smile, handsome face, and hot body out of her mind.

"I can't, Kiana," Owen took a sip of his wine. "You know I have to be up nearly all night."

"Mmm," Kiana grinned as she straddled his lap, deliberately letting her short dress ride up high on her thighs. "I am sure I can help you with that."

Owen stared into Kiana's eyes and swallowed. His pupils dilated as his body instantly responded to hers. Her soft lips met his for a gently teasing kiss that trailed along his jawline to tickle his sensitive ear.

"Kiana," Owen's voice was hoarse as he breathed her. "You know I can never say no to you."

Owen's hands grabbed her, pulling her closer to him so his mouth could crush hers as his desire for her overtook all his reasoning. He turned and flipped her onto her back on the sofa, and her legs wrapped around his waist.

"You are so beautiful," Owen whispered before, once again, melding his lips to hers.

Kiana's legs tightened around Owen's waist, and her arms locked around his neck as she moaned when his lips left hers to travel down her throat and trail over her collarbone. Before his head could dip any further, his phone rang. He took a deep breath to steady himself.

"Don't answer it," Kiana's voice was throaty with desire as she tried to pull him back on top of her.

"I have to," Owen smiled at her apologetically before picking up his phone and walking onto the balcony to take the call.

"He just up and left after his phone call?" Magda pulled the ice cream from the bag before finding two spoons in Kiana's kitchen drawer. "What an idiot." She plopped down next to Kiana on the sofa.

"Owen is the least of my worries right now." Kiana leaned forward and picked up the letter her boss's secretary had dropped off an hour ago, a few minutes after Owen had left.

"Patrick fired you?" Magda took a spoon of ice cream as she scanned the letter. "This is what happens when you kiss the boss at Christmas parties, then turn down his date invitations." She put the letter down on the table before taking another scoop of ice cream.

"I am sure that is not why I was fired," Kiana shook her head at her friend. "The company has not been doing too well lately, so they are letting a lot of staff go."

"Well, maybe you should have gone on a date with him then," Magda said seriously. "I know how hard it was for you to find this job and how much you need it."

"I am not sure what I am going to do now," Kiana took a spoonful of the ice cream. "I have my rent due in a few weeks, and I still need money to send back home."

"I can help you," Magda hugged Kiana. "Don't worry. We will figure this out somehow."

"Could this week get any worse?" Kiana threw her hands up in despair.

"You know what I think we need?" Magda asked. "I think we need to go out for a drink or two."

"I think you may be right about that," Kiana said without hesitation.

"I like this bar," Kiana sipped on a glass of red wine. "How did you find it?"

"One of my regular customers told me about it," Magda raised her glass before taking a sip of her wine. "She said it is where everyone who is anyone goes."

"Ah," Kiana smiled. "So you mean it's where the snobs go!" They laughed.

"I think she means it's where you meet all the eligible bachelors," Magda eyed out the room. "I think she was right. Most of the people in here are wearing clothes that would cost me six months to save up for."

"I do feel a little underdressed!" Kiana rolled her eyes. "But this house wine is a lot better than the house wine at our usual bar."

"That's because it is twice the price," Magda pulled a face.

"I am going to go powder my nose," Kiana put on a posh voice. "I will have another one of this great wine if you get the waiter's attention."

"Server," Magda corrected Kiana. "I think that is what their job titles are now."

"Great," Kiana shook her head and shrugged before she walked off.

Kiana scrolled through her phone as she made her way back to the table. She was not looking where she was going when she rounded the corner and walked into a warm wall of muscle. She dropped her phone.

"I am so sorry," Kiana said, bending down to pick up her phone, not taking any notice of the man she bumped into.

"Kiana?" a deep voice said above her.

Kiana froze; the last time she heard that voice was right before she had thrown up on him. She pinched her eyes shut, hoping it was her imagination playing tricks on her. When she opened them and looked up, Ronan was standing and smiling at her.

"Hi," Kiana said, slowly standing up and nervously fiddling with her dress.

"Imagine bumping into you here?" Ronan smiled at her. "Are you okay?"

"I am fine," Kiana gave him a shy smile. "I am sorry about bumping into you and the whole throwing up all over you!"

"You did kind of make a mess on me," Ronan laughed. "How is your head?"

"Better," Kiana nodded.

"Can I buy you a drink?" Ronan asked her.

"I am here with my friend," Kiana told him.

"That's good because I'm here with my friend too," Ronan told her. "Maybe we could all have a drink together?" Ronan asked, hopefully.

"Your friend. Do you mean Dr. Baxter?" Kiana asked him thoughtfully.

"Yes," Ronan looked at her curiously. "Why?"

"I think my friend took quite a shine to Dr. Baxter," Kiana grinned. "Why don't you both join us at our table?"

"Great," Ronan gave a little bow. "I will go and get us some drinks and Hayden."

"Dr. Gorgeous is here?" Magda asked, immediately fiddling with her hair. "He is coming to sit with us?"

"Yes, and yes," Kiana laughed. Magda seemed overly nervous. "You like the doctor!" she accused.

"What?" Magda fobbed her off. "I think he is gorgeous and intelligent."

"Uh-huh," Kiana sipped on her wine. "All right then."

"How are you feeling seeing Ronan again?" Magda asked Kiana. "Did he manage to get all your lunch out of his hair?" Magda laughed and dodged the napkin Kiana threw at her.

"Here they come," Kiana felt like a teenager as that feathery feeling tickled her stomach again.

"Hi," Ronan's eyes met and held Kiana's. "You remember Hayden?"

"Yes, of course," Kiana smiled at Hayden. "This is Magda. Magda, this is Ronan.

"Good to see you again, Magda," Hayden's voice dropped slightly before turning back to Kiana. "How are you feeling, Kiana?" Hayden smiled down at her.

"I am feeling a lot better, thank you," Kiana assured Hayden.

"You still remember your appointment next week?" Hayden raised his eyebrows at Kiana questioningly.

"I have not forgotten," Kiana assured him, but her eyes kept locking with Ronan's.

CHAPTER 3
The Day After the Night Before

"Would you like to come for a nightcap?" Ronan asked Kiana after Magda and Hayden had left them.

"A nightcap where?" Kiana asked him.

"My place?" Ronan smiled at her hopefully. "I live right around the corner."

"This is your neighborhood?" Kiana was impressed. "Of course, it would be," she laughed, looking at his expensive wristwatch.

"This way," Ronan steered her towards his apartment building. "Welcome to my home."

"I love your apartment. It has a great view," Kiana stood on the balcony, her shoulder brushing against Ronan's. "I bet you don't even look at it anymore."

"I often sit out here in the evening and have my quiet time," Ronan smiled.

"I can see why you have your quiet time out here," Kiana looked up at him.

Her eyes locked with his, their smiles faded, and the world around them melted away. Ronan and Kiana both took a step toward each other. No words were spoken. None were needed as their chemistry drew them together. Ronan's hands lifted, cupping her face and pulling her lips towards his. Their lips touched, and they drew back; their eyes were dark with passion as they stared at each other. Kiana swallowed. Her heart felt like it was trying to hammer its way out of her chest. Her lips tingled, wanting more of his. She reached up, hooking her arms around his head, and pulled his lips back to her. The spark flickering between them burst into flames as the kiss deepened. Ronan lifted her, and she wrapped her toned legs around his waist. He turned and walked her into his bedroom.

Ronan's phone buzzed beside his bed. His hand patted the bedside table next to him for his phone.

"Hello," Ronan mumbled into his phone.

"Mr. Waters?" the doorman's voice echoed in his ear.

"Yes," Ronan yawned, willing himself to wake up.

"The senator stopped by and left a letter for you, sir," the doorman informed Ronan. "If you don't mind, I will send Mindy up with it."

"Sure," Ronan rolled his eyes. "Leave it in the usual place."

Ronan hung up the phone and then turned over, expecting to find the beautiful Kiana. Instead, he found a note on the pillow, and her perfume still scented his pillow. Ronan felt cold, let down, and hurt.

He had not been able to get Kiana out of his mind since he had scooped her up off the gym floor. Both the manager of the gym and Hayden were not forthcoming with information about Kiana. Ronan could not believe his luck when he bumped into her the previous night.

Ronan was hoping to wake up feeling her lithe warm body beside him. Instead, he woke up to cold empty sheets and a thank you for last night's note. She didn't even leave her number for him to contact her. But they had spoken a lot during the evening, and he knew a lot more about her.

Ronan smiled, lying on his pillow and staring at the ceiling. What was it about Kiana that had him all twisted up inside? He had his fair share of women in his life. They had come and gone without so much of a fuss or a second thought from him. But Kiana had stuck in his mind and inflamed his body with longing.

Ronan smiled, his eyes closing as he let his mind drift back over the previous night.

"What do rich men like you do each day?" Kiana lay curled in Ronan's arms, and her fingers idly stroked his chest.

"Work," Ronan laughed at her mock shocked expression. "What? Did you think I slept all day and partied all night?"

"Yes," Kiana grinned, kissing him.

"What do you do all day?" Ronan asked Kiana.

"Run my boutique," Kiana started to kiss his chest, making him lose his train of thought. "I try to get home as much as I can to help out my father with my brother and sister."

"And your mother?" Ronan's breathing became labored from Kiana's teasing lips.

"She passed away when I was fourteen. My little brother was four," Kiana sighed and rolled over onto her back. "That was the worst year of my life."

"I'm sorry," Ronan turned onto his side, lying on his

17

elbow to look at her and link his fingers through hers. He wanted to touch her and feel her close. She was driving him crazy. "I lost my parents when I was young too."

"Oh?" Kiana turned and looked at him. "I'm so sorry. I could not imagine what it would be like to lose both parents."

"It was a long time ago," Ronan gave Kiana a sad smile. "My uncle stepped in and raised me. He and his wife never had children of their own."

"That was admirable," Kiana moved closer to Ronan.

"So, tell me about your boutique," Ronan said, wrapping his arms around her and pulling her closer.

"I started it a few years ago after I stopped modeling," Kiana sighed, closing her eyes and enjoying the feel of his lips on her skin. "I sell clothes from up-and-coming young designers as well as a few top designer names."

"What does your father do?" Ronan asked her, his body once again starting to crave hers.

"Ahh," Kiana's breath caught in her throat as Ronan's lips traveled over her collarbone, and his fingers worked their way lower down her body. "He is a retired military officer."

A banging on his bedroom door had Ronan sitting up straight in his bed with fright.

What the hell? Ronan rubbed his hands over his face before wrapping the sheet around his body and setting off to murder whoever was banging on his bedroom door.

"So, you are still alive?" Hayden raised an eyebrow.

"What the hell are you banging on my bedroom door for?" Ronan glared up at Hayden, who topped Ronan's six-foot-two frame by at least two to three inches.

"Uncle Bruce called me to ask me if I knew where you were," Hayden turned and walked towards the kitchen, saying over his shoulder. "You missed your lunch date with him."

"Lunch?" Ronan asked, confused, his eyes falling on a letter propped up on the side table.

"Yes," Hayden started to gather items together for coffee. "Lunch!"

"What time is it?" Ronan's eyes widened when he glanced at the clock on the wall. "It's two o'clock already?"

"Uh-huh," Hayden took two coffee mugs from the cupboard. "I take it you had a late night last night?" He grinned.

"Some of us didn't have surgery at first light," Ronan said sarcastically. "And besides, it's Saturday. I always sleep in on the weekends." He turned back towards his bedroom. "I'm going to jump in the shower. You know how I like my eggs."

"Sure, I will make your brunch for you," Hayden shouted after him. "I'm hungry anyway, and we all know you can't cook."

"That was a great meal, just what the doctor ordered," Ronan smiled mischievously at Hayden. "You should have been a chef and not a surgeon."

"Cooking relaxes me. If it were a job, it would stress me out," Hayden picked up his bottle of beer. "I take it you had quite the night."

"You know a gentleman never kisses and tells," Ronan grinned, having another cup of coffee. "You could also have been a barista." He ducked the bottle cap Hayden threw at him. "What? You have incredible skills in the kitchen. You are going to make some woman a great husband one day."

"Now you sound like your uncle," Hayden rolled his eyes. "How long has Uncle Bruce been on us to settle down?"

"Since we reached puberty, I think." Ronan shook his head before sitting back in his chair and saying earnestly, "Do you ever think how different our lives would have turned out if our parents weren't gunned down?"

"I think we would still have had Uncle Bruce's influence in our lives," Hayden took another sip of his beer. He had learned to turn his emotions off a long time ago. "He was always the stabilizing element even before the death of our parents."

"I still have nightmares of that day," Ronan said softly. "It hits me when I least expect it."

"I told you years ago to go see someone," Hayden leaned forward on the table. "You promised me you would." He frowned at Ronan.

Hayden's birthday was only seven months before Ronan's. But they had been raised by the same uncle in the same home, and Hayden had assumed the older brother's role.

"Do you think Uncle Bruce will ever tell us what our parents were involved in that got them assassinated?" Ronan fiddled with his coffee cup.

"Have you ever asked him?" Hayden started to pull the label off the beer bottle.

"Have you?" Ronan countered.

"No," Hayden pursed his lips, shook his head, sat back, and took a sip of his beer. "I don't think I want to know."

"How do you do that?" Ronan's eyes narrowed in on Hayden.

"Do what?" Hayden frowned at Ronan.

"Just sweep it all away as if nothing happened." Ronan shook his head. "Even after everything we went through, you were like marble."

"Honestly," Hayden looked at Ronan. "It was either shut down or break down. You were in pretty bad shape, so breaking down was not an option. Especially with our only living relative in critical condition in the hospital, and Rosa was falling to pieces."

"Really?" Ronan looked surprised. "I thought Rosa was so together."

"No," Hayden shook his head. "She put on a good face because you were badly hurt, both physically and emotionally. She knew you needed her."

"We needed her," Ronan corrected him. "You lost your parents at the same time that I lost mine, and like me, you witnessed what happened to them."

"Yes," Hayden nodded. "But I handle trauma differently, unlike you. I compartmentalize emotions and actions, which is why I am such an excellent surgeon." He grinned.

"You always have to find a way to shove the excellent surgeon into the conversation, don't you?" Ronan sighed. "That article about you has gone to your head, buddy."

"Well, I was tired of reading about the great exploits of international playboy Ronan Waters," Hayden laughed at the pained expression on Ronan's face.

CHAPTER 4
Another Day, Another Lecture

"It is nice of you to join me today," Bruce Waters drawled sarcastically to Ronan.

"You know Saturdays are my morning after the night before," Ronan grinned when his uncle rolled his eyes at him.

"At least with Hayden, I know he is probably in surgery or consultation," Hayden grimaced. "With you, I have to hope that no policeman knocks at my door."

"Oh, come on," Ronan defended himself. "I'm not that bad. And you always play favorites with Hayden."

"Well, he is the only one of my two nephews that bothers to call and excuse himself if he has to miss one of our family meetings," Hayden laid on the guilt.

"Okay," Ronan gave up. "I'm sorry, Uncle Bruce, but time slipped away from me yesterday."

"What he means is," Hayden grinned cheekily at Ronan's warning look, "he was up until the early hours of Saturday morning and promptly slept the rest of the day away." His smile broadened at the look of relief on Ronan's face.

"When are the two of you going to find nice young ladies

to settle down with and give me more nieces or nephews?" Bruce sighed. "Is it too much to ask to want to see you both happy and content with your lives? Instead of philandering and then sleeping your days away?"

Ronan and Hayden were Bruce's nephews. Ronan was Bruce's brother's child, while Hayden was his late wife Amy's younger brother's child. Both Hayden and Ronan lost their parents the same day Bruce lost Amy and his unborn baby.

Bruce swallowed. He still had nightmares about that horrific day. Not a minute of a day went by that Bruce did not worry about his nephews. He thought of them as his sons. Even before losing their parents, Ronan and Hayden lived at the Waters family estates with Bruce and Amy.

Their parents had been friends and business partners that had traveled a lot for work.

When Bruce's political career started taking off, he and Amy hired Rosa, a young au pair who doubled as Hayden and Ronan's tutor, chef, and best friend. She soon became part of the Waters family, running their household and caring for everyone, including Bruce and Amy.

It was Rosa that had saved the three of them on that day. She had done everything she could to save Amy, but the bullet that had struck her had severed an artery. Bruce could not unsee the look on Rosa's face from that day. Her eyes were wet with tears, and her cheeks were smeared with blood as she fearlessly protected her family.

"Uncle Bruce?" Ronan snapped his fingers. "Taking an afternoon nap there, old man?" He laughed.

"Don't be rude, Ronan," Bruce snapped at him. "I hope you boys both remember what day it is tomorrow."

"Monday," Ronan gave Bruce a cheeky grin. "Of course, we remember, uncle." His expression became more serious. "How could we ever forget!"

"Therapy?" Hayden beckoned a waiter. "I'm starving. Can we order?"

"God, you are always hungry," Ronan widened his eyes at Hayden. "Where do you put it all, though? I mean, you are like a six-foot-four eating machine."

"Six-five," Hayden corrected proudly. "I have a fast metabolism." He grinned.

"Yeah, roadrunner speed fast," Ronan laughed, eyeing Hayden's lean well-defined build. "Even as kids, you could pack any kind of food away without putting on an inch."

"You're just jealous that I always got picked first for basketball," Hayden gave Ronan a cocky grin. "Oh, and volleyball. Do you remember the summer in Fort Lauderdale?"

"Oh, yeah!" Ronan sat forward, cupping his drink. "That was a great summer." He stopped and turned towards Bruce, whose eyes had narrowed into slits. "Well, it was a great summer until uncle party pooper here came and dragged us home."

"You were sixteen," Bruce raised his eyebrows.

"I still cannot believe Rosa turned us in like that," Hayden frowned.

"It wasn't Rosa," Bruce's face turned up into a half-smile. "It was the security detail I had tailing you. They had orders to yank you out as soon as they saw a threat."

"Security detail?" Hayden and Ronan said at the same time.

"Of course," Bruce told them matter-of-factly. "You don't

get to be the nephews of a politician without having twenty-four-seven security tailing you."

"You could have told us," Ronan's brows drew together. "That also explains a hell of a lot." He looked at Hayden.

"You're right," Hayden gave a small laugh. "The Dooley boys. Their mysterious disappearance after that night in Reno."

"Yes, and those cowboys in Arkansas," Ronan's eyes widened as he turned to Bruce. "You don't have details on us still, do you?"

"You boys are men now," Bruce shrugged noncommittally before changing the subject. "Now, back to the subject at hand. The memorial service tomorrow is going to be quiet and secure, as usual."

"I have no appointments or surgeries scheduled for the day," Hayden informed Bruce.

"I took a long weekend and am only due back in the office on Wednesday," Ronan told his uncle. "But then, being my boss, you already knew that." He sighed.

"Waters Real Estate and Construction is now your company, Ronan," Bruce shook his head. "I am now merely a member of the board."

"Of course you are," Ronan tilted his head. "Who is catering the memorial tomorrow?"

"Rosa has the new chef at the manor doing it," Hayden told them. "Mother does not want any strangers in the house. She has become even more paranoid these past few months." Hayden took a sip of his wine. "Which you would both know if you came to visit her more often."

"Hint taken," Ronan held up his hands. "I was there a few weeks ago."

"Three months ago, Ronan," Hayden corrected him. "You were there for her eightieth birthday."

"That was three months ago?" Ronan pulled a face. "Huh, time does fly."

"You are no better, Hayden," Bruce looked at his older nephew. "You were at the manor eight weeks last."

"What?" Ronan looked at his uncle. "Do you have some sort of biometric scanner that scans our comings and goings from the manor?"

"Speaking about that," Bruce leaned forward. "You both need to have your biometrics done tomorrow, or you will not be able to get into your apartment building, the office, or the manor."

"You're joking, right?" Hayden nearly choked on his wine. "First full boot-camp combat training camps twice a year. Then keycard controls and tracker apps. Now you're going biometric?"

"Hayden," Bruce raised his eyebrows. "You cannot be too careful these days."

"Is there something you are not telling us?" Ronan looked at his uncle suspiciously. "Margaret, your secretary, did mention you were updating all the security and asked for mine and Hayden's phones." Ronan looked at Hayden. "I need your phone, by the way."

"I believe so," Hayden shook his head. His uncle could be overly paranoid at times. His paranoia seemed to increase at this time of the year. "I will drop it off at your apartment later today."

"Great," Ronan smiled to himself.

His uncle may be a bit overprotective, but installing a new app on Hayden's phone meant having access to his contacts.

This was one security update that Ronan did not mind doing. Ronan grinned smugly.

"So," Bruce sat back as a waiter came to take their order. "What are we going to eat today?"

They ordered and settled back into the ping-pong-type conversation about when Hayden and Ronan would settle down. Their uncle wanted one of them to take over the manor and raise their family there. He had even suggested there was plenty of space for more than one family, and they could subdivide the estate.

Hayden and Ronan had often discussed living on the estate. They were sure that prisoners locked up in high security would have more freedom than living in the manor. Their uncle had told them when they had turned eighteen about their parent's assassination. It was then that they learned the incident at the restaurant had not been a random shooting. It was a targeted hit made to look like one.

Ronan was still curious about his and Hayden's parents' deaths. As far as they knew, their parents were in the real-estate business. They sold properties all over the world. It never made sense to him why they would be targeted. Uncle Bruce, however, Ronan could understand being targeted. His uncle was heavily into politics at the time. He still was, being a United States senator. But Bruce had assured him they were not after him.

Bruce and granny Dora were tight-lipped about that day and what happened or why it happened. All Ronan and Hayden were told was that they were safe, not knowing the details.

CHAPTER 5
The Cold Hard Truth

"I have been to five job agencies and sent my résumé to ten companies today," Kiana flopped onto Magda's sofa. "Thank you so much for letting me stay in your spare room."

"I should have thought about this long ago," Magda handed Kiana a glass of white wine. "It is kind of nice having a housemate again."

"I am sorry all my stuff has taken over your garage," Kiana breathed, thinking about the move. "I really don't know what I would do without you."

"Let's not find out then," Magda winked at Kiana. They had been friends for as long as she could remember. "I have been thinking about an interim job for you."

"Oh?" Kiana took a swallow of the wine.

"You don't have to worry about paying rent or food for a while," Magda explained. "But, you can work at the boutique for money to send home. I can't pay you much, but you can earn a good commission."

"Seriously?" Kiana looked at Magda wide-eyed. "You would do that for me?"

"Of course," Magda smiled at her. "Gosh, if it were not for you, I would have been bullied all throughout school."

"Those kids needed a serious attitude adjustment," Kiana said, thinking back to their school days.

Magda's parents were environmental lobbyists who refused to support large corporations and hated wastefulness. Both of Magda's parents were from wealthy families, but they made their own clothes and grew their own food. As a result, Magda was always teased. It did not help that she was also a shy, gawky kid.

"Have you told Owen yet about your move?" Magda asked.

"I did, on the day I moved over here," Kiana frowned and bit her lip. "He sent me back a thumbs-up emoji."

"Really?" Magda looked confused. "That does not sound like something Owen would do. Has he ever sent an emoji before?"

"Not that I can recall," Kiana looked at her friend, perplexed. "I am not even sure if we are still together. The last time I saw him was last Friday, the night we went to that new bar."

"That was five days ago," Magda looked shocked. "What is wrong with the guy?"

"He has been acting strangely for a while now," Kiana moaned. "Working late nights, weekends, and taking on heavier caseloads."

"I can remember when you first started dating. Owen could not leave you alone for more than a few hours at a time." Magda poured them some more wine. "I actually thought he was a bit too possessive, especially for a free spirit like you."

"Yes," Kiana pulled a face. "He was a bit suffocating at first. But so, so sexy."

"He is sexy," Magda agreed. "There is no denying that; his nerdish manner makes him even more so."

"Have you got a crush on my boyfriend?" Kiana teased Magda.

"Oh, goodness, no," Magda looked horrified. "He is not my type of nerd at all."

"No, but I think Dr. Gorgeous is," Kiana grinned as Magda's cheeks reddened. "I have never seen you so girly around a man before."

"He is kind of special," Magda said dreamily. "And ever so intelligent."

"And emotionally unavailable?" Kiana asked her friend. "Magda, you know that you and Hayden are too alike, right?"

"What is that supposed to mean?" Magda looked a little hurt.

"Ever since Todd, you go for men that you know are emotionally distant," Kiana took Magda's hand. Her eyes were dark with sorrow. "You know he would want you to be happy, right?"

"I know," Magda wiped a stray tear from her cheek. She could not believe that even after five years, just the mention of his name could make her weep. "Todd was a special guy whose life ended way too soon."

"He was a great guy," Kiana smiled.

Todd Rogers was the all-around boy next door with a great smile, an army of friends, and the Lacrosse team captain. He had grown up on the same street as Magda and Kiana. His parents, Kiana's parents, and Magda's parents had all been good friends. Until their final year of high school, the three of them were nothing more than good friends. The summer before their last year, Magda and Todd had gone to the same summer camp, and it was there that they had fallen in love.

During their second year of college, Todd became terminally ill. Magda and Todd decided to get married and spend what little time Todd had left together. What Magda did not know was that Todd had made sure she was well provided for.

The house Magda lived in was the one Todd had bought for her a few weeks after being married.

"Hayden is different," Magda fixed her mind on the present. "He is sweet, kind, and a little guarded."

"I think it is more than a little," Kiana said. "Although he does have a great bedside manner."

"I would not know," Magda's cheeks again went red. "We have not progressed to that part of the relationship yet."

"Yet?" Kiana's smile grew. "Oh, my word." Kiana breathed. "You really do like him, don't you?"

"I think so," Magda scrunched up her nose. "What is not to like?"

"Yes, tall, blonde, and handsome!" Kiana raised her glass in salute to her friend. "And a doctor. If your parents were still alive, they would most definitely not approve."

"Heck no," Magda shook her head.

Magda had loved her parents, but she had often pretended that Kiana's father was her father. Kiana could not understand why anyone would want the sergeant major as their father. He had been strict and rigid, well up until his accident, that is. After that, he started to mellow a bit. No more army tours meant having to take a desk job and not spending long periods away from his kids.

Kiana's mother was also military, so she and her siblings were raised by their grandmother, who lived with them. When Kiana was fourteen, her mother was killed in action. That was not a good year for Kiana. She had gotten into endless amounts of trouble and became a teenage rebel. She had joined some of Magda's parents' causes and ran away from home a few times. That was the year she dyed her hair pink and blue, went against her grandmother and father's wishes, and got a tattoo. She had even tried some pot. The worst thing about that year was that she had dragged loyal Magda through the mud with her.

Todd had been their saving grace, pulling them out of their rebellion phase. After that year, Magda blossomed; her body filled out, her skin cleared up, and she turned into a beauty. She was no longer shy or awkward. But Magda was not the only one who had blossomed. Kiana, too, had grown into her looks and had become a beauty. The two of them turned heads wherever they went.

"I am still so sorry about your parents," Kiana's brows drew together. "They were not your standard parents, but they were good people."

"No, they were definitely not your average mom and dad, that's for sure," Magda grinned. "Do you remember that time my mom tried to teach us to sew?"

"Yeah," Kiana laughed. "I sewed the bedcovers to the pillowcase."

"And I embroidered my skirt in with my embroidery," Magda and Kiana giggled. "Mom was not impressed."

"But back to the future," Kiana looked at Magda. "When do you want me to start?"

"How about tomorrow after you go and see Owen at his office?" Magda suggested.

"Why would I do that?" Kiana asked Magda.

"Because you need to sort out whatever is or is not happening between the two of you," Magda told her. "I know you, Kiana Bridges. That way, you can decide what to do about that dreamy blue-eyed real estate mogul who keeps messaging you."

"You know about that?" Kiana eyed Magda suspiciously.

"I'm your best friend," Magda patted Kiana's hand. "There is not much I don't know about you." Magda grinned. "If I am honest, I much prefer Mr. Brown Eyes to Owen, the dull dictator."

"I can't wait much longer," Kiana stood up, glaring at Owen's assistant. "I am going through."

"No," Sally got up and tried to stop Kiana. "I don't think you should go in there now."

Kiana eyed the woman who had stood up to block her way down the passage to Owen's office. She looked genuinely concerned but not about Owen; Kiana had a feeling the concern was for her.

"Sally, please move out of the way," Kiana stepped around the woman and stormed to Owen's office.

As Kiana's hand touched the door handle, she heard soft laughter and what sounded suspiciously like a moan of pleasure. Shockwaves tingled up Kiana's spine as anger and adrenaline spurted through her veins.

What the heck was going on in there, she thought, bursting into the room, then freezing at the sight of Renee perched on Owen's lap.

"Owen!" Kiana hissed as more shockwaves coursed through her. "I knew it!" She ripped the necklace he had given her for her birthday off her neck, tossing it on the ground before pivoting and storming towards the exit.

"Nice workplace you have here," Kiana sneered at Sally as she grabbed her coat on the way to the elevator.

"Kiana," Owen called after her. "Wait, please, it is not what it looks like."

Kiana ignored him and stepped into the lift, managing to get the doors to slide shut before he could reach her.

"That cad," Magda said, hotly handing more tissues to Kiana. "You always suspected there was still something between Renee and Owen."

"Right there in his office!" Kiana hiccupped between sobs.

"I don't even know why I am crying." She tossed another tissue in the bin.

"Even though you suspected it, it is a big shock finding out it was true," Magda said gently. "You know what?" Magda stood up. "Let's close up early and get some ice cream and junk food on the way home. We can put on our PJs and have a good girly night of weeping and bad-mouthing Owen."

"I think I would like that," Magda sniffled.

"Then tomorrow when you have had a chance to sleep on it," Magda picked up Kiana's phone. "You can message that sexy blue-eyed Ronan and tell him you will meet up with him after all."

"I don't know if I am ready for that just yet," Kiana wiped her eyes. "Besides, he thinks I am some ex-model boutique owner with a military officer father."

"Well, your dad is a military officer," Magda said soothingly. "So not everything was a lie."

"Yes," Kiana hiccupped. "But you know my dad does not do all the official ceremonial stuff officers of his stature normally do."

"So," Magda shrugged, "that does not make him any more of a decorated officer than he is."

"I know, but I think it is time for a completely fresh start," Kiana said shakily, helping Magda lock up after Chloe shot off once they knew they were closing early.

"You know you can put it right with Ronan," Magda said gently. "You thought it was a one-night stand. Who tells the truth when you have a one-night stand?" She shrugged. "Remember Theo? He still thinks I am a pilot who does long-haul flights and is never in one city long enough to have a relationship."

"Oh, yes," Kiana laughed. Magda always knew how to cheer her up. "Poor Theo, excellent-in-bed-but-far-too-clinging Theo."

"Yes," Magda's eyes grew wide. "Him."

"But he was just a one-night stand," Kiana sighed. "If I start something with Ronan, I have a sneaky suspicion it may turn into more. And I don't feel like another Bex."

"Agh," Magda grimaced. "I thought we were not allowed to mention the B-word?"

"He left me standing at the altar," Kiana hissed. Anger burned through Kiana's stomach.

"I still cannot believe that man dared to cash in the honeymoon, get the money back for the reception, and take off with it all." Magda had sworn if she ever bumped into Baxter Grant, she would punch him in the face.

"It destroyed us," Kiana hissed. "Not only did he break my heart and humiliate me, but he also cleared out my father's savings account and Tammy's medical fund account."

"I hope the authorities eventually found him," Magda locked the boutique. "And that he is rotting in some prison somewhere."

"My father nearly lost everything," Kiana pinched the bridge of her nose. "All because I fell in love with a bad boy who was also a con artist."

"Kiana, you have to stop beating yourself up over Baxter," Magda linked her arm with Kiana's as they walked off towards the store.

"My father cannot retire when he had planned to," Kiana stressed. "He is even considering selling the house because Tammy's medical bills are so high."

"Hopefully, this round of treatment will be the last for a while," Magda said optimistically. "That poor girl has been through so much already."

"I hope so too," Kiana grabbed a box of her favorite cookies. "Can we add these?"

"Of course," Magda put another box in the basket. She had a feeling they were going to need it.

CHAPTER 6
Finding the Will to Go On

"Kiana, please let me help you out," Magda argued with Kiana. "You can pay me back when you start to earn again if that makes you feel better."

"I can't take that kind of money from you." Kiana sobbed. "I will not do that to our friendship."

"It is not for you," Magda tried to convince Kiana. "It is for Tammy."

"I will have to take that hotel job," Kiana blew her nose. "It is the only way."

"Fine," Magda said. "Take the hotel assistant manager job. Although you are way too overqualified for it."

"I cannot worry about qualifications right now," Kiana pushed her disheveled hair out of her eyes. "Tammy's procedure has been moved up a month. I have to find a way to get the deposit for it to my dad."

"You know what?" Magda picked up her phone. "I am just going to pay it anyway. I have the money to spare, and Tammy is my sister too."

"No," Kiana tried to grab Magda's phone. "I can't let you do that. My father will kill me."

"Your father won't know," Magda held Kiana at bay. "There, it is done."

"Thank you," Kiana hugged Magda before punching her on the arm. "That is for going against my wishes."

"Ow," Magda rubbed her arm. "Now I can't wear my strappy dress on my date with Hayden." She went over to look at her arm in the mirror. "You know how easily I bruise."

"You and Hayden have been out a lot over this past month," Kiana grinned at Magda. "That is the longest you have been in a relationship in five years."

"I know," Magda's face turned dreamy. "He is magnificent."

"Uh-oh," Kiana looked a little shocked. "I know that look."

"What look?" Magda frowned at Kiana.

"You are falling or have fallen for him," Kiana accused.

"What?" Magda looked at Kiana. "No, I just like him ... a lot!"

"Uh-huh," Kiana nodded. "If I am not mistaken, I think the sexy doctor feels the same way about you. His emotions have become available to one Miss Magda Drake."

"What about you and Ronan?" Magda asked, moving the topic onto Kiana's love life. "When will you show up for one of your meetings with Ronan? It has been nearly a month since you split up with Owen."

"I thought about meeting him tonight," Kiana surprised Magda by saying. "That is why I asked if I could borrow your blue dress."

"Yes, that is a great choice. That color is gorgeous on you," Magda's eyes lit up. "Come; let's get you ready for your date."

"We have hours before my date," Kiana laughed at her crazy friend.

"Then let's go grab some lunch and then come back and get us both ready for our dates tonight," Magda said enthusiastically.

"Why are you not at the boutique today?" Kiana asked Magda, suddenly realizing it was a Friday.

"Chloe is running the shop today," Magda told her. "After you and she had a falling out and you left us, I had to bribe Chloe to stay by offering her more responsibility and half of what I was paying you like a raise."

"I have to grudgingly say that Chloe is an excellent salesperson," Kiana admitted. "I am sorry I walked out on you like that. You gave me a job, and I just messed it all up."

"Oh, don't worry about it," Magda waved it off. "Mrs. Jackson needed to know she could not squeeze her fat butt into a size two."

They laughed, but it had been a horrible day that day. Kiana had just got the news that Tammy's procedure was going ahead a month earlier, which meant the hospital needed a deposit to secure her spot. Her father still did not know that Kiana had been fired, and Joey's tuition was also due soon. Kiana was on edge and did not have time for a fat lady trying to squeeze herself into a pair of jeans two sizes too small for her.

When Kiana got home, she had even contemplated taking an overdose of sleeping pills. At least her life insurance was still valid, and that would have solved all her family's problems. But then Kiana remembered the clause in her policy that they did not cover suicides, and she did not have any pills either.

"I could have a yard sale and sell all my furniture and household stuff," Kiana said as they prepared for lunch. "When last did we have a yard sale?"

"When you tried to sell off your father's stuff so we could go for spring break to California?" Magda told her.

"Yeah," Kiana pulled a face. "Not one of my best ideas."

"No," Magda shook her head. "But if you want to sell all your stuff, I don't mind having a yard sale. I even have an attic full of stuff to donate to the cause."

"Well, that's settled then," Kiana felt better about Magda helping her out thinking about the yard sale. If she could get enough, she could pay Magda back and send money home for Joey's tuition.

"How about in two Saturdays?" Magda asked. "That will give us enough time to sort out the attic and the garage, price things, and advertise."

"Wow," Kiana laughed. "You are a miss entrepreneur, aren't you?"

"If you are going to do something, you may as well do it right," Magda shrugged. "Besides, this is for a good cause. We want to get the most out of all the items we are going to sell."

Kiana smiled as she watched and listened to Magda list everything needed for the yard sale.

"Now I feel like I have gained about five pounds," Kiana complained as they walked back into Magda's house that they now shared. "But that dessert was fantastic. Oreo cheesecake with salted caramel is my new favorite dessert."

"I think the entire restaurant noticed when you had two huge servings," Magda shook her head at Kiana. "You and your sweet tooth."

"Well, my saving grace is my one-year free membership at the gym," Kiana told her, not feeling at all guilty about eating all that cheesecake. "But I do feel like I need to sleep for a few hours, though."

"Oh no, you don't," Magda waved her finger at Kiana. "You are not getting out of your date tonight." She warned Kiana. "I know your 'oops, I overslept' routine, missy."

"Now that I have had time to think about it," Kiana grumbled, "I don't think starting up any kind of a relationship right now is good for me. I am just not in the right place at the moment."

"Stop it!" Magda said forcefully. "You are going on that date tonight if I have to stuff you in the trunk of my car and drag you there."

"Well, that's not a disturbing image," Kiana looked at her friend wide-eyed.

"I mean it, Kiana," Magda warned Kiana. "You have been moping around for a little over a month now. Promising Ronan you would meet him, then not showing up." She marched Kiana to the shower. "He is not going to stick around for much longer with you standing him up all the time."

"Okay, I get the point," Kiana sighed. "I will go and not stand him up this time."

"Great," Magda grinned. "Now, let's go start getting ready. I think tonight I may be the one that stays out!"

"You go, girl," Kiana grinned, turning on the shower. "Are you and Dr. Gorgeous getting a little serious?"

"I do feel differently about him," Magda told Kiana. She pulled a clean fluffy towel from the bathroom closet and put it on the towel rail. "Don't use all the hot water! I want to wash my hair. I'm going to choose something to wear."

Kiana turned and watched Magda swish into her bedroom. She smiled. Kiana had not seen her friend this happy in years. Kiana's grin faded. She just hoped Dr. Gorgeous and his unemotional heart did not break Magda's.

"You look fabulous," Magda assured Kiana. "Now get out of my car and go meet Ronan. You are going to make me late."

"I'm sorry," Kiana took a deep breath. "I am not sure I am ready for this."

"We are not going to go over this again!" Magda raised her eyebrows at Kiana. "You've got this, now go get him." She leaned over Kiana and opened the door. "Now scoot before I get a fine. I don't want to be late for my date."

"Fine!" Kiana complained, climbing out of the car. "What if I want to leave?"

"Here," Magda dug in her purse and pulled out fifty dollars. "Cab fare."

"Great, thank you!" Kiana shook her head. "Now I feel like a call girl."

"A costly one in that dress," Magda grinned. "Now go, and you know you can always call me if you need to."

"Thanks." Kiana gave Magda a tight smile. "Love you. And be safe."

"Love you too." Magda blew Kiana a kiss, pulled the door closed, clicked her seatbelt back in, and pulled off before Kiana could change her mind again.

"Oh well," Kiana stood there watching Magda's taillights fade into the distance. "I guess I am here now, so I may as well go in for one drink." She said to the air.

"Kiana?" Ronan's deep voice made goosebumps pop up on her skin.

Kiana slowly turned around. Shoot, now there was nowhere to run, and she was already in trouble if just his voice made her feel all warm inside.

"Hey," Kiana gave him a small smile and waved.

"I was about to call you," Ronan smiled at her. "You look gorgeous." He cleared his throat.

"Thank you," Kiana told him shyly. "Why were you about to call me? I'm not too late, am I?"

"No," Ronan assured her. "You are right on time. I have to go and sort out a problem with one of my overseas deals. I was going to ask you to meet me at my place instead. We could order in if you don't mind?"

"Sure," Kiana's heart started to pound at the thought of being alone in his apartment with him once again.

"Okay, great," Ronan turned and hailed a cab for them.

Something inside Kiana's stomach turned, and an overwhelming feeling that everything was going to work out washed over her. The feeling grew stronger when she climbed into the cab, and Ronan's tall warm body slid in next to her. She was glad Magda had forced her to meet Ronan tonight.

CHAPTER 7
The Sleepover

"You speak German?" Kiana was impressed.

"I speak a few languages," Ronan told her, stretching out his long legs in front of him. "I have had to learn. The company is international, and my translators are not always available at the hours I need them to be."

"A man of many talents," Kiana smiled at him seductively.

"Have I told you how beautiful you look tonight?" Ronan turned towards Kiana, moving closer to her. "I am happy you turned up this time."

"I'm sorry about the other times," Kiana looked into his eyes and felt as if she was being pulled towards him. "To be honest, I had just come out of a relationship that did not end very well."

"That is all you had to say to me," Ronan moved closer, his hand reaching out to cup the side of her face. "I would have understood."

"I know," Kiana put her hand over his. She wanted him to pull her closer. "I was afraid that if I did, you would stop calling." She said honestly. "And I didn't want that to happen."

"I don't think I could have stopped calling you, Kiana," Ronan's voice was gruff as his head dipped forward and his lips covered hers.

Kiana's arms circled his neck and pulled him closer to her. Their kiss got deeper as their passion ignited, and Kiana turned to straddle Ronan's lap. His hands slid up her bare legs to draw her as close to him as he could get her. His body was on fire for her. She was all he could think of these past three weeks and the only woman he wanted warming his bed.

Holding her, Ronan flipped them over so Kiana was lying flat on her back on the couch with him on top. His lips wanted to taste all of her. While his need for her made the rest of the world around him fade away. His hands shook with desire as he dragged the straps down on her dress. His lips were about to follow the path of the clothing he pulled over her soft skin when the elevator buzzed.

Ronan pinched his eyes shut and tried to think of things that would have the same effect as a cold shower on him, but all his mind could think of was Kiana.

The elevator buzzed once again.

"I believe that is our food," Ronan's voice was gruff as he pulled away from Kiana, pulling her straps back into place.

"I had forgotten we even ordered food," Kiana cleared her throat and sat up, pulling her clothes straight and fixing her mushed hair as best she could.

"Thank you for leaving a bit of cheesecake for me," Ronan laughed, taking the last bite of the dessert. "You were not lying when you said you loved this dessert."

"What can I say?" Kiana grinned. "I have a terrible sweet tooth."

"My sweet tooth is for you," Ronan's eyes caught and held

Kiana's as his head moved closer to hers. "I have to satisfy this craving I have." He smiled sexily as his head dipped, and his lips caught hers.

She tasted like cheesecake and red wine, and her body curled into his when he pulled her closer. They were sitting on the floor in front of the coffee table, which he pushed away with one arm. Not letting go of her, Ronan flipped Kiana onto her back.

He straddled her, leaning on his hands and knees, staring down at her. His eyes were dark with lust. He lowered himself gently on top of her. His mouth traveled from her lips to her soft silky throat with its exotic perfume. Ronan's hands found the straps of her jewel blue dress. He skillfully maneuvered the shoestring straps off her shoulder to expose the prize his lips were seeking.

Kiana moaned. Her body arched into his teasing mouth. The movement almost pushed Ronan over the edge. He closed his eyes and drew in a deep breath to steady himself. He felt like an inexperienced teenager with Kiana.

"Will you stay the night?" Ronan's lips moved back towards Kiana's, making her whimper.

Their eyes met, mirroring their desire and need for each other.

"Yes," Kiana whispered. Her head reared up so she could feel his lips on her once again.

"Will you be here when I wake up?" Ronan pulled back teasingly once again.

Kiana swallowed. She looked up at him while her body ached for his.

"Kiana," Ronan whispered, "tell me I will wake up with you in my arms tomorrow morning." He almost pleaded with her.

"Yes," Kiana whispered, her arms snaking around his neck. She pulled her head up to crush his lips with hers.

"What time is it?" Kiana asked Ronan as she stretched out her aching muscles.

"Just after two," Ronan turned to her and smiled. "How about a shower?"

"How about sleep?" Kiana laughed. They had made love at least four times already that night.

"Shower, then sleep," Ronan smiled at her, drawing herself closer to him. He started to kiss and caress her again.

Ronan did not know what had come over him. She was like a drug in his system that he could not get enough of. She had bewitched him, gotten under his skin, and made him a slave to his desire for her.

"Okay," a soft, throaty moan escaped Kiana's lips as his skillful hands touched all her sensitive spots. "Let's go shower." She turned and kissed him, her hands greedily gliding over the firm, defined muscles of his back.

Ronan was furious that he had to take a call precisely when he was about to step into the shower with Kiana. He downed a quick glass of whiskey.

What the hell was wrong with him? He had never been like this over a woman before! He could not get enough of her.

He heard the water still running in the shower and grinned. Taking a deep breath, he walked into the bathroom.

He pulled off his shirt and shorts as he watched her body move with the water in the shower. He felt his instant desire for her flesh over him as he opened the shower door.

The water belted down the perfect curve of her back. Her hair was up in a bun showing off her swan-like delicate neck. Ronan's lips longed to touch, and his tongue watered to taste the soft curve of it. He swallowed and stepped into the shower. Kiana tried to turn around to face him, but he stopped her, trapping her hands up against the shower wall. Ronan's head dipped, and his lips caressed the back of her neck, his tongue snaking out to lick and tease as his mouth dropped lower onto her shoulders to nip and tantalize.

His rock-hard body pushed against her, and he once again almost came undone when she let out a throaty whimper.

"Kiana," Ronan was hoarse with his need as his hands rounded the front of her body and pulled her back onto him.

"Please, Ronan," Kiana's voice was rough with longing as she pushed her head back, wanting to feel his entire body against hers.

Ronan could not remember ever having a night of passion as he had done that night with Kiana. It was past four o'clock in the morning before they finally fell asleep wrapped in each other's arms.

As Ronan drifted off to sleep, he toyed with the thought of locking the door to make sure she was still there when he woke up. But he dismissed that thought, thinking it to be a little creepy. A smile lingered on Ronan's lips as he dropped into a dream filled with Kiana.

Ronan stretched lazily, his arm reaching out for Kiana only to hit a cold empty sheet. He sat straight up in bed, the sheet floating down over his naked torso as his eyes scanned his room.

Kiana was nowhere in sight. His heart pounded in his chest, and disappointment felt like someone had punched him in the gut. He pulled the sheet around his waist before rushing into the living room. His heart nearly stopped at the sight in front of him.

Kiana stood with her back to him, filling the coffee machine as the most delicious smell of cooking awoke his hunger. She had one of his business shirts that were way too big for her; it engulfed her body like an oversized dress that sat just above her knees.

Ronan moved forward quietly. A smile spread across his face, and his heart kicked into overdrive as he heard her humming softly. He stopped a few feet away, just staring at her. Ronan could not help it. He felt as if he could stand here watching her the entire day.

"Morning, beautiful," Ronan said softly, grinning when she spun around, grabbing her chest in freight.

"Good grief, you move like a cat," Kiana breathed with fright. "Sorry, I hope you don't mind that I started to make us something to eat. I'm starving."

"Yes," Ronan gave her a knowing smile. "After all our exercise last night, I think we are both starving." His eyes told her he was talking about more than food.

CHAPTER 8
A Weekend With Ronan

"Hey there, stranger," Kiana answered her phone when Magda called. "How are you? Sorry I have not been home yet."

"Oh," Magda laughed softly, and Kiana could picture her blushing. "Neither have I been home since last night." She whispered.

"Mmm," Kiana grinned. "So, is this official now?"

"I think so," Magda sounded like a teenager with her first love. "He is wonderful. We spent most of the night talking and ..." She cleared her throat. "And you know ..."

"You mean having sex?" Kiana said the s-word and then laughed, knowing that Magda's cheeks would be flaming now.

"I would call it making love," Magda said seriously. "It was sensuous, exciting, but it was more ... like we were connecting on a deep emotional level." She sounded a little afraid.

"Okay," Kiana picked up on the slight panic in Magda's voice. "That is a good thing, Magda." She said softly. "It means Dr. Gorgeous means more to you than the other flings you have had over these past five years."

"If it is a good thing, then why do I feel like I just betrayed Todd?" Magda's voice dropped.

"No," Kiana's voice firmed a little. "Don't go there, Magda. Todd would have wanted you to feel again and have another great love. He will always be your first. What do you always tell me?" Kiana asked her. "Love never dies. It just takes on a different form."

"I feel like Todd is fading from me," a catch in Magda's voice made Kiana think there was a lot more going on that Magda was telling her.

"Todd will always be your first love, and no one can replace that, Mags." Kiana soothed. "Do you want to tell me what is really going on here?"

"You know me so well," Magda gave a shaky laugh. Kiana could picture her wiping away her unshed tears. "Dr. Gorgeous wants me to meet his family next week."

"Ah," that made sense, Kiana thought. "That means he has let down his wall, Mags, and that is huge."

"I don't know if I am ready for that," Magda told Kiana. "It is just moving too fast."

"You can slow it down anytime you want to, Mags," Kiana's voice was gentle. "Explain how you feel. I am sure he will understand."

"He asked me to spend the weekend with him at his beach house," Magda told Kiana.

"Are you going to accept his invitation?" Kiana asked her.

"I don't know," Magda's voice held a hint of fear and confusion.

"Why don't you go but take your car?" Kiana suggested. "That way, if you feel uncomfortable at any time, you can leave, and you will feel better knowing you have an escape plan."

"You do know me so well," Magda laughed. She sounded a

lot more confident. "Thank you. I love you. Be safe," she said before hanging up.

"Everything okay?" Ronan asked Kiana as he walked out onto the balcony carrying two glasses of white.

"Oh, just girl stuff," Kiana gave Ronan a slow smile, lifting her face to receive a kiss before he gave her the wine.

"You should not have let me doze on the couch," Ronan cricked his neck. "Now my neck is all out of place."

"You seemed like you needed it," Kiana took a sip of the wine. "Especially after I beat you in three out of four of your video games."

"You cheated and distracted me with your womanly wiles," Ronan grinned back at her.

"No, I did not," Kiana defended her gaming titles. "I won those games fair and square." She took another sip of her wine before squinting at him. "Do you want a rematch?"

"I think we should get some dinner as it is almost seven, and then I will challenge you to a rematch." He gave her a slow sexy smile, letting her know precisely what kind of rematch he had in mind.

"I look forward to it," Kiana's lids drooped seductively as her teeth worried her bottom lip.

"What would you like for dinner?" Ronan's voice became husky as he watched Kiana fold her bare legs beneath her while she curled up on the deck chair.

"Pizza?" Kiana could not remember the last time she had a pizza.

"Pizza it is then," Ronan said softly, his eyes trailing hungrily up her legs where his shirt dipped slightly to show off her naked skin. He swallowed, took a sip of his wine, cleared his throat, and then stood up to go find a pizza menu before food became the last thing on his mind once again.

Kiana's throat felt dry as she watched Ronan stand up. His lean muscled torso was shirtless and made her fingers itch to touch every contour of them again. She sighed. They had spent the whole day half-naked in his apartment, playing games, watching television, dozing, and making love.

Ronan has asked her to stay one more night, and she agreed to do so, along with promising to be there when he woke up this time and not in the kitchen. She smiled, her heart skidding when he told her she had nearly given him a heart attack to find her missing from his bed that morning.

Kiana saw Ronan beckoning to her from the living room. She stood up and walked inside to join him and pick a pizza for their dinner. Once that was done, they curled up on the sofa and chose an action movie to watch while they waited for their pizza. They did not see much of the film. Once again, their desire for each other consumed them.

Their pizza arrived at an inconvenient time, and Kiana thought Ronan would murder the pizza delivery guy. The poor teenager had brought up the wrong pie and had to go all the way back down to get the correct one.

Once again, they laughed and talked about random stuff while they ate their pizza, made incredible love, and then curled up to try and watch their action movie once again. Kiana fell asleep, nestled against Ronan's warm hard body, only to find him carrying her to bed when the movie was over.

Kiana woke up to the gentle caress of soft lips, kissing her throat while a hand skillfully caressed and kneaded her yearning flesh. A small moan rose in her throat as she whispered Ronan's name.

Ronan's body moved on top of hers, and his lips found hers as their bodies joined.

"I can't get enough of you, Kiana," Ronan's voice was pained. "You are driving me crazy." He whispered in her ear before the world exploded around them.

Kiana smiled as a warm hand caressed her arm, and soft kisses floated upon the back of her neck and down her spine.

"Good morning, sleepyhead," Ronan's husky voice purred into her ear as his lips moved to her cheek, and then he turned her over and pulled her when he rolled onto his back. "I could wake up like this every morning." He sighed, gently playing with her hair.

"Mmm," Kiana said sleepily as her hand idly caressed his chest.

"Will you stay here a few hours longer, just lying here like this?" He asked her.

"Mmm," Kiana said again as she drifted back to sleep. "Just like this," she mumbled.

"I will catch a cab home quickly and meet you at the restaurant in two hours," Kiana told Ronan. "That way, you can make your calls, and I can go home, shower, and get some fresh clothes."

"I don't know if I can be without you for that long," Ronan held her beneath him on the sofa where they had just made love for about the fourth time that day.

"The time will fly by, and you know you need to make that call you have been avoiding this weekend," Kiana reasoned with him before rolling out from underneath him.

"Yes," Ronan sighed, running his hands through his hair. "You are right."

"I am going to get dressed and go," Kiana kissed him. "I will meet you at the restaurant at eight." She grinned, dodging his hand that reached out to grab her.

Ronan had offered to drive her home, but she did not want him to know where she stayed. She still had not told him the truth about herself, that she did not own a boutique, that she had never been a model, and that her life sucked right now.

Kiana knew if their relationship kept progressing as it did, she was going to have to tell him the truth about herself. That worried her as he would know her as a liar and someone who had cheated on her boyfriend.

Kiana needed to chat with Magda and ask her for advice because now she knew she was falling for Ronan. She felt so alive when she was with him. Their bodies, minds, and souls seem to have entwined. Kiana just hoped that Ronan could forgive her for lying when he found out the truth, and Kiana knew she had to tell him tonight, but she needed to speak to Magda first. Kiana reasoned it was best to get advice before diving headlong into ripping off the Band-Aid and telling someone you had been intimate with you were a raging liar.

CHAPTER 9
Meeting the Family

"How did the second interview go?" Magda asked Kiana as she dropped her purse on the coffee table before plopping onto the sofa.

"It went well," Kiana told her friend. "I will know by the weekend if I got the position."

"I will repeat this." Magda yawned. She was exhausted. "You are way overqualified for that job, but I am glad you may get it as a stopgap to finding a better one."

"Thank you," Kiana got up to get Magda a coffee. "Are we all set for the yard sale on Saturday?"

"Yes," Magda perked up a little. "Chloe is going to look after the store, and I will be here with you. We have had quite a response to my adverts already. A lot of the stuff is booked."

"Oh, that is good news," Kiana put two cups of steaming coffee on the table before curling up next to Magda on the sofa. "I may be able to pay back sooner than I expect."

"How about paying me back a bit and getting yourself some nice work clothes?" Magda suggested. "Start a new job with a new attitude."

"Have you decided to go meet the relatives tomorrow night?" Kiana asked Magda.

"After a wonderful weekend at his beach house," Magda reached for her coffee, "I have decided to go to meet the family."

"Eeehhhhh," Kiana wiggled on the sofa excitedly. "I am so glad. This is huge for you." Kiana hugged Magda.

"Don't spill that hot coffee on me," Magda warned Kiana, watching her flap the coffee cup around. "And, yes, it is huge for me."

"What time are you leaving tomorrow?" Kiana asked Magda.

"I am going to meet Hayden right after I have closed the boutique," Magda told Kiana. "I have to take an overnight bag as we will probably be staying over."

"That is great," Kiana was so happy for Magda. "Ronan asked me to stay over tomorrow night at his place because Thursday is a holiday."

"Ah," Magda smiled. "So we will both be absent from home base then."

"Seems so," Kiana nodded, taking a sip of her coffee. "I think I have fallen in love with Ronan."

Magda nearly choked on her coffee as she turned to look wide-eyed at Kiana.

"Well, that was just thrown in there from nowhere," Magda said, surprised. "But I am not surprised; the two of you make the air around you sizzle. You are so hot for each other."

"Another rather disturbing imagery from you," Kiana told her friend. "But you and Dr. Gorgeous have just as much chemistry. Just in a more confined sort of way."

"You mean we don't burn everyone in our orbit up with our flaming desire for each other like you and Ronan," Magda laughed.

"It is true. We cannot keep our hands off each other,"

Kiana frowned. "I worry that maybe when all the passion dies, I will find I was in lust with him and not in love with him."

"Oh, Kiana," Magda sighed. "I have never seen you so twisted up over a guy before. Not even the B-word, we are not allowed to say." She gave a soft whistle. "And the B-word had you so starry-eyed, you could not see straight."

"So, you think I do not see straight with Ronan?" Kiana's eyes narrowed in on Magda.

"No," Magda held up a defensive hand. "I did not say that. I merely meant that not even Baxter had made you look like you do right now. You are glowing, and your whole attitude has changed. It is like you float everywhere you go now."

"Thank you, I think!" Kiana eyed Magda strangely. "Have you been drinking?" She grinned when Magda hit her with a pillow.

"What should we have for dinner tonight?" Magda asked her. "I feel like Chinese."

"Nah." For some reason, the thought of Chinese made her stomach roll. "How about if I made a nice green salad with some grilled chicken?"

"You are feeling a lot better," Magda looked Kiana over. "That sounds awesome. I will help you with the salad."

"No," Kiana shook her head. "You go take a nice, long bath. I know it is a stock take for you, and you have been working long hours. Go relax, and I will take care of dinner."

"Thank you," Magda signed contentedly. "You are a life-saver." She blew Kiana a kiss before padding off to go and run a nice hot bath to rest her weary body in.

"Where are we going?" Kiana asked Ronan as they sped into the countryside in his luxury car.

"To my uncle's place for dinner," Ronan grinned at her. "I told you we were invited to dinner and to spend the night."

"No," Kiana raised her eyebrows at him. "You said to pack some clothes so I could spend the night and that we were going out to dinner."

"Exactly," Ronan gave her another cheeky grin.

"I wish you had told me," Kiana grumbled. "I am not very good with families."

"You will do fine, and trust me on this," Ronan turned into a small road lined by endless farmland. "My uncle is going to love you."

"I wish you had better prepared me," Kiana was not impressed.

She was even less so when Ronan turned in front of large black gates that screamed to everyone on this side of them that they held a mansion inside their boundaries.

Ronan punched in a code on the gate keypad, and they started to swing open. He looked at her, taking her hand encouragingly and kissing it.

"You are going to be great," he assured her before squealing up the drive.

"Isn't that Hayden's car?" Kiana asked when Ronan pulled up beside a black Jaguar.

"I believe it is," Ronan confirmed. "Did I forget to mention they would be here too?"

Kiana's heart dipped.

"Wait," something dawned on Kiana. "Hayden said he was taking Magda to meet his family. Does that mean the two of you are related?"

"Not by blood, no," Ronan explained. "My uncle Bruce was married to Hayden's aunt."

"Was?" Kiana looked at Ronan curiously as he pulled their bags from the trunk.

"Yes, she died the same day as both mine and Hayden's parents did." His voice dipped, and he gave her a tight smile.

Kiana turned and gulped as she stared up at the imposing mansion staring down at her.

"You grew up here?" Kiana pointed to the stately manor house.

"Yes," Ronan sighed. "It was not as fun as you might think it would be."

"No," Kiana shook her head sarcastically. "Not at all. Poor you!"

"Come on," Ronan started up the stairs to the front door. "Let's go get settled."

"I feel like I am checking into a hotel," Kiana muttered, following Ronan.

The front door flew open, and a beautiful woman ran out, grabbing Ronan in a big hug.

"There you are," her voice had a Latin tilt to it, matching her beautiful long dark hair and dark eyes. "You must be Kiana." The woman turned to greet Kiana warmly. "Come in, come in."

"Hi," Kiana smiled at the woman feeling a little more relaxed.

"I'm Rosa," the woman introduced herself. "I run this museum for this ungrateful bunch." She laughed when Ronan rolled his eyes at her.

"Rosa has been mine and Hayden's keeper since we were about five," Ronan explained to Kiana.

"Yes," Rosa pinched Ronan's cheeks. "And I know all his secrets." She kissed his cheek fondly. "Now, come on. Put those bags down there. Danny will take them up to your rooms in a bit. Come, come, your uncle is waiting with Hayden and his beautiful lady friend. You have both made him so happy this day." Rosa talked so fast she was making Kiana's head spin.

"Ah," Bruce stood up from the sofa where he sat next to Magda when Kiana and Ronan walked into the living room. "You must be Kiana." Bruce walked up to hug her like he had known her for years. "I am so glad to finally meet you. Come sit; have a drink."

The thought of alcohol made her feel a little nauseous. She had not been feeling too well lately and thought she was coming down with the flu.

"Could I possibly have a club soda, please?" Kiana asked politely.

"Of course," Bruce nodded and then walked off to go take care of her drink, greeting his nephew on the way.

"Your uncle is Bruce Waters?" Kiana hissed at Ronan.

"Didn't I tell you that?" Ronan pulled a face. "Sorry, I thought I had mentioned it."

"Again," Kiana raised her eyebrows at Ronan. "You did not."

"Gosh, it is so good to see you," Magda stood up and walked to Kiana. "I feel so out of my depth. I feel as if my parents are looking down at me, judging me." She whispered into Kiana's ear.

"Oh, yes," Kiana nodded, looking wide-eyed at her friend. "From what I have read about the senator's politics, they really would not have been happy." Kiana and Magda stifled their giggles.

"Kiana," Hayden came over and handed her a club soda. "You are looking well."

"Thank you," Kiana greeted him. "I am feeling well," she lied; the smell of Magda's wine made her feel like she might be getting sick on her shoes. "Sorry, is there a bathroom I could use?" She asked Ronan softly.

"Of course," Ronan was about to lead the way when Rosa popped up.

"I will show her the way," Rosa grinned. "You need to go

and see gran; she is not feeling too good, and Hayden has put her on bed rest." She glared at Hayden.

"What?" Hayden looked down at Rosa. "Her blood pressure is way too high, and I don't like the swelling of her sprained ankle."

"Gran sprained her ankle?" Ronan looked a little alarmed. "Will you excuse me, Kiana? Rosa will show you the way. I must go to see my gran."

"Of course," Kiana needed to get to the bathroom fast. Her stomach was not feeling good. It must also have been the trip. She never was very good with road trips.

"This way, my dear," Rosa stood aside for Kiana to walk through the door.

CHAPTER 10
Everything Can Change in a Second

Kiana was grateful to Rosa for taking her up to the room made up for her. There would be no sharing rooms unless you were married or at least betrothed in the Waters household.

Who even uses the word betrothed these days? Kiana wondered, splashing water on her face after having been violently ill. She wandered through to the bedroom. It was gorgeous, better than any hotel suite Kiana had ever been in. Not that she had been in many hotels, but she and Owen had done a few short holiday weekends away.

Owen? Kiana shook her head. Why had his name popped into her mind? Kiana had nearly forgotten he had even existed in this past week. She had been too caught up in a whirlwind romance with Ronan to even give him a second thought. She opened the cool fresh bottle of water that had been placed on a tray on the dresser. She felt a lot better but still wished her body had not picked this particular week to get the flu.

She took a deep breath, straightened up her outfit, and was heading out of the door when there was a soft knock.

"Who is it?" Kiana called.

"Ronan," Ronan's head popped through the door. "Hi." He said as he snuck in and quietly shut the door behind him. "I needed to see you." He stepped up to her. "Did you brush your teeth?" He leaned in for a kiss.

"Yes," Kiana breathed, returning his kiss. "I was feeling a little gritty from the drive."

"Mmm," Ronan growled, pulling her closer. "I missed your body curled next to mine the last few nights." He told her softly; their kiss turned more passionate as Kiana's arms curled around his neck.

"Your uncle is going to wonder where you are," Kiana's voice was gravelly with passion.

"Let him wonder," Ronan lifted her and walked her over to the bed. "He has taken Hayden, Rosa, and Magda to see the horses."

"I want to see the horses," Kiana moaned as Ronan went to work undressing her.

"Mmm," Ronan said again as Kiana helped him out of his shirt. "We can catch up in a bit." He said as his body covered hers.

"Thank you for the lovely meal, Bruce and Rosa," Kiana said as Ronan pulled out her chair for her.

"You are welcome, my dear," Bruce said kindly. "I take it you four are going to enjoy a nice stroll around the garden then?"

"I was going to show Magda the carriage room," Hayden looked at Ronan. "She wants to see the old dresses and antiques in there."

"Of course," Bruce nodded. "Just remember to check on gran before you retire for the night." Bruce stood and wished them all goodnight before he left them to get some work done.

"Well, goodnight, you two," Hayden gave Ronan and Kiana a knowing grin. "We will see you bright and early for breakfast." Hayden and Magda left them.

"Come on," Ronan took her hand and pulled her through the house and out of a large glass sliding door, where he stopped to pick up a basket and blanket. "I want to show you something."

It was a beautiful evening as they ran through the garden, past a line of trees to pop out around a beautiful lake that reflected the moon's silver light.

"It's beautiful," Kiana breathed while Ronan put down the basket and spread out the blanket.

"I thought you might like it," He grinned before pulling him down beside him on the blanket. "I used to come to fish here when I was a boy."

"Did you ever catch anything?" Kiana stretched out next to Ronan.

"A few colds maybe, but never any fish," Ronan laughed. "I'm glad you came here with me tonight." He said softly, lying back with his head propped on his hands.

"Thank you for bringing me," Kiana leaned on one arm, looking down at him.

Her heart had done a flip-flop when he had introduced her to his grandmother as his girlfriend just before they went down for dinner.

Their eyes met and held as a soft breeze teased her hair. Ronan reached up to twirl a soft lock around his finger.

"You are so beautiful," Ronan breathed with his eyes filling with desire as her head lowered to his.

Without breaking their kiss, Kiana straddled Ronan and slowly slid her length out along his. Her body instantly reacted to his sharp intake of breath and low moan as she gently wiggled against him before he growled and rolled her over.

"You little vixen," Ronan breathed, letting his lips seek out all her tender spots.

Their passion ignited once again, and they tore at each other's clothes. Both of them were desperate to feel the other's skin against theirs.

"I love you, Kiana," Ronan breathed as he lost himself in her.

"I love you too, Ronan," Kiana cried out.

The world around them faded, leaving only the two of them locked in a delicate dance of love.

Kiana's world seemed a lot brighter this morning. She had gone from despair and a broken relationship to falling madly and passionately in love with a man like Ronan Waters.

They had left the manor around nine that morning, and as it was a beautiful day, Ronan wanted to take her for a picnic at the beach. He said they needed to talk, and what better place to do that than at the beach?

Kiana's stomach was in knots. Ronan had told her more than once during the night that he was in love with her. She could not believe it! She was so happy that she felt like she was going to burst.

Ronan pulled up in front of his apartment building.

"I will just rush up and get a few things," Ronan told her. "I will be back in a few minutes. If the police come, just take the car around the block."

"Okay," Kiana smiled as he leaned in for a kiss before rushing into the building.

The lift doors were closing when she heard a phone bleep. She found Ronan's phone had fallen between the seats. She picked up as the phone bleeped again.

It could be his work. Kiana thought, picking up the phone

only to feel the world suddenly go ice-cold around her. A face of a beautiful woman pulsed on his screen. She sat there staring at it until the call switched off. Within the next few seconds, a whole string of messages appeared.

Kiana's head spun. She felt as if someone had taken her heart in a vice grip and squeezed until it popped. She could not say if she was hurt, angry, or both, as she felt utterly numb except for the pins and needle feeling in her hands. She threw the phone down on the floor.

Kiana did not care that his keys were in the car. Nor was she waiting around for him to explain why Valerie was asking where he was. And she honestly did not want to know why Valerie was missing his naked body in her bed. All Kiana could think of was getting out of there and running away as far as possible from him.

Why did this keep happening to her? Kiana's mind reeled while hailing down a taxi.

On the entire way to Magda's house, the last few days with Ronan played over and over in her head. Were all the calls he got in business class? Or were they Valerie wanting him to warm her bed for her? Kiana, though nastily.

Her phone rang, making her jump. She looked down at it and saw it was Ronan. She hit reject, then turned off her phone.

All men were alike. Kiana thought. She would not cry; no, she would not! This was the last straw. Kiana was swearing off men for a long, long time.

There was no one home, and Kiana felt oddly relieved. Usually, she would have run straight to Magda and cried on her shoulder. But instead of crying, Kiana felt nauseous and dizzy. She ran to the bathroom and got violently ill. When Kiana was finished getting sick, she had a shower, brushed her teeth, put on her comfy PJs, and went to binge-watch soap operas on television.

When Magda came home later that night, she found Kiana fast asleep on the sofa with a pile of used tissues beside her while the television played some old black-and-white movie.

Uh-oh! Magda thought Kiana had once again landed up with a broken heart. Anger flared through Magda. She was going to find Ronan and give him a piece of her mind. One minute he was confessing his love for Kiana, and the next, Ronan was breaking her heart.

Magda left Kiana sleeping on the sofa. Tomorrow was going to be a tough day for Kiana. She would need her sleep tonight.

CHAPTER 11
A New Job

It had been two weeks since Kiana had run off from Ronan. He had tried to call her on numerous occasions. He had even called Magda, but Kiana refused to take his calls and blocked his number from her phone.

Two days after the incident with Ronan, Kiana started her new job as assistant manager at one of the city's top hotels. If she were honest with herself, she would have to admit to liking her new position. Kiana was learning a lot about the hotel industry, which she found out she had a real passion for. The biggest bonus of all was the lovely people she was working with. Even her boss was such a great man, and he was happily married, so Kiana did not have to worry about him trying to date her like her previous boss.

"Simon?" Kiana knocked on his office door. "I am going to take off for the day if that is okay."

"Ah, Kiana," Simon looked up as Kiana walked into his office. "Please, come in. The Parrys wanted to thank you for helping them with their son, but you were taking care of the food orders."

"Oh, that was sweet of them," Kiana said, already feeling as if she had been working at the hotel for years.

"My dear, are you feeling okay?" Simon asked her worriedly. "You seem a little pique."

"I'm fine," Kiana lied. "Just a little tired and trying to get used to my new work schedule."

"Well, you are already doing such a fine job, Kiana," Simon told her honestly. "Now go home and get some rest," he ordered her.

"Please, please," Magda begged Kiana. "Hayden is away at a medical conference, and I want to attend this gallery opening." Magda held up the exclusive tickets a customer of hers had given her.

"Agghhhhhh," Kiana moaned. "I have a splitting headache, and I have to get up early for work tomorrow." She pretended to bang her head against the wall. "But as you did such a good job with my yard sale last weekend, I guess I owe you." She sighed.

"Yay," Magda clapped her hands together gleefully. "Come on; let's go see what to wear." Magda pushed Kiana towards a rack she had brought home from the boutique.

"You brought home some of your boutique dresses?" Kiana looked astounded.

"Not just any dresses," Magda said mysteriously. "My new line of Jenny Lynn, who personally asked me to stock them."

"You're joking," Kiana's eyes grew wide. "Magda, this is huge for you."

"I know!" Magda could not contain her excitement.

Magda pulled the sheet she had covered the rack with off to reveal the most beautiful array of dresses Kiana had ever seen.

"Oh, my," Kiana felt like she was magically pulled towards the rack.

"I know," Magda fingered the delicate material of one of the dresses she particularly liked. "She has given me the choice of two to keep, and I want you to have one of them."

"Seriously?" Kiana looked at Magda wide-eyed. "I don't know what to say."

"Think of it as an early birthday present," Magda told Kiana.

"I had nearly forgotten about my birthday," Kiana gave Magda a tight smile. "I don't much feel like celebrating it this year."

"You can't let dictator Owen and douche Ronan ruin your special day," Magda told her. "We are going to celebrate, and I think I know just the place to go celebrate."

Kiana felt like a princess in the beautiful jade green strappy Jenny Lynn dress and matching shoes. Magda had chosen the classic little black dress style, only it was not black but ruby red, which Magda always looked so stunning in.

"Oh, this place is gorgeous, Magda," Kiana stood holding a glass of champagne that she had hardly sipped.

Once again, the smell of the wine, or most alcoholic drinks for that matter, made her feel sick. For some reason, the wine had become quite pungent and acidic smelling to her, almost like she was sniffing a bottle of vinegar.

Kiana thought she might have an ulcer from all the stress and anxiety she had been under these past seven or eight weeks. Even her head was fuzzy, and she forgot silly things she should remember. She would go and see the doctor next week as she had Tuesday off from work.

"It is Sammy Blunt's gallery," Magda linked her arm

through Kiana's as they walked around the magnificent gallery admiring the artwork.

"Kiana?" A familiar male voice had Kiana's shoulder stiffening. "I thought that was you."

Slowly she turned around with Magda still glued to her arm.

"Owen," Magda gave him a scathing look. "I never took you as one for the arts."

"Sammy is my cousin," Owen explained. "I am here supporting her."

"Figures," Magda glared at him.

"Do you mind if I have a word with Kiana," Owen glared at Magda, "alone?"

"It's okay," Kiana gave Magda a small smile.

"I won't be far away if you need me," Magda gave Owen a warning look before reluctantly walking off.

"What do you want, Owen?" Kiana's eyes narrowed in on him.

"You look fantastic," Owen swallowed as his eyes darkened with desire. "I have been trying to contact you. I even went to your apartment, but you had moved out."

"I blocked your number," Kiana told him and was not forthcoming with information about where she had moved.

"Kiana, please, you have to believe me that Renee means nothing to me," Owen reached for Kiana, but she took a step back.

"Really?" Kiana looked at him blankly. "That is not what I saw in your office that day."

"You took off so fast you did not give me a chance to explain," Owen ran his hand through his hair nervously. "Renee and I had been out to lunch. We had had a little too much wine, and then in the office, she tripped and fell onto my lap." He swallowed. "I was a little tipsy, and we just kissed. That is all."

"Sure," Kiana nodded. "You know, Owen, I don't care how it happened or why. The fact is something did happen." She sighed. "I can never trust you again, and I don't need the complication in my life right now." Kiana put her drink down. "Now, if you excuse me, I think it is time for me and Magda to leave."

"Please, Kiana," Owen reached out and grabbed her arm. "I will do anything for you to give me another chance. I miss you so much."

"I think Kiana told you we were leaving," Magda stepped between them, breaking Owen's hold and Kiana's arm.

"Please call me," Owen ignored Magda. "Let's talk this through."

Kiana took her coat from Magda, and without a backward glance at Owen, she left the gallery.

"Do you think I was too hasty in dumping Owen?" Kiana asked Magda as they made some hot chocolate when they got home from the gallery opening.

"No," Magda shook her head. "Definitely not. I never liked him, and I still don't."

"He seems like he genuinely misses me," Kiana sipped her sweet drink.

"Don't even go there," Magda warned her. "You are just setting yourself up for disappointment with that man all over again."

"I know," Kiana sighed. "I guess I'm just feeling a little lonely. You have Dr. Gorgeous, and all I have are my pillow and soap operas."

"You have a new job that you seem to be loving," Magda was as surprised as Kiana was that she was enjoying her new job.

"I guess," Kiana shrugged, settling comfortably on the sofa. "Shall we watch the movie?"

"Yup," Magda pulled some of the blankets over her as they settled in to watch a sappy movie.

CHAPTER 12
Kiana's Special Day

Kiana could not concentrate properly at work the next day. Her mind kept wandering back to her meeting with Owen the night before. He had seemed genuine about his feelings for her, and if she was honest, she cheated on him as well with Ronan.

So much had happened recently that Kiana could not believe it had been almost eight weeks since she had had her one-night stand with Ronan. Kiana would love to blame her downward spiral on that night. But the fact was, her life's downward spiral had started long before then.

"Kiana," the young woman at the front desk called to her. "There is a man on the phone for you. He says he is your father."

"My father," Kiana looked at her, alarmed. "Thank you. Can you put it through to my office?" She turned and headed to her office, closing the door behind her.

Kiana had dreaded telling her father about losing her job, but he had surprised her by asking her why she hadn't just come home. Her father had finally gotten his promotion and was now in a higher pay bracket with a lot more benefits to go with it. According to Kiana's brother Joey and her sister Tammy, her father was seeing a new lady friend. Kiana smiled, thinking it was about time. Her father had not dated since he had lost his wife.

"Hi, Dad," Kiana said worriedly. "Is everything okay? I was going to phone later to find out if Tammy is ready for her operation next week."

"Honey," her father's deep voice echoed through the phone. "We called you to say happy birthday."

"What?" Kiana frowned. Kiana glanced at the calendar. Good grief, she had forgotten her birthday. "Thank you, dad." She grinned, hearing her younger sibling singing to her in the background. "Thank you, Joey and Tammy." She called through the phone. "I love you all too."

Kiana's heart sank as she realized how much she was missing her family.

"I can't wait to see you guys on the weekend," Kiana told them, suddenly realizing her trip home was this weekend if today was her birthday. How could she have forgotten that? Her memory has been like Swiss cheese lately.

"Okay, honey," her father said. "We will let you get back to work. We hope you have a great day. Don't work too hard."

Kiana dropped her head onto her desk after she hung up the phone. She felt drained. Kiana was so exhausted. She was physically, mentally, and emotionally near the end of her tether.

Her mobile phone rang. She looked down at it, not recognizing the number. She frowned, wondering if she should answer it or not.

"Hello?" Kiana said into the receiver.

"Hi," Owen's voice came from the other side of the phone. "Please don't hang up." He begged her. "I wanted to wish you a happy birthday and ask you if you would have dinner with me tomorrow night."

"I'm sorry, Owen, but I am going home for the weekend with Magda, and we are leaving early tomorrow," Kiana told him.

"Are you busy tonight?" Owen asked, hopefully.

"Owen, I'm sorry, but I'm not doing this with you right now," Kiana's head started to throb.

"Meet me for one drink," Owen pleaded. "One drink, that is all I ask."

"Fine," Kiana looked at her watch. "I finish work in two hours. I will meet you at the usual place."

"I will be there," Owen said softly before hanging up.

Kiana sighed. What had she done?

"Thank you for meeting me," Owen smiled at Kiana. "I ordered you a white wine."

"Actually," Kiana beckoned the waiter. "I would prefer a club soda."

"Uh," Owen looked a little taken aback. "Sorry, I should have asked."

"Yes," Kiana looked at him. "You should have."

"Did I do that a lot?" Owen asked her

"Yes, you did," Kiana decided to tell him the truth. "I hardly ever had a say in anything during our relationship."

"I'm sorry," Owen looked genuinely apologetic. "I have been going over our relationship repeatedly in my head. I cannot believe how I treated you. I am sorry."

"What am I doing here, Owen?" Kiana could not help it. She still had a lot of anger toward him.

She knew that more than half of her anger was not even aimed at him. But he was there, and Ronan was not, plus she had not caught Ronan in the act as she had Owen. Kiana deserved a little retribution.

"I wanted to give you this," Owen pulled a box out of his pocket. "Happy birthday, Kiana."

She eyed him with narrowed eyes before taking the present and opening it. In the box was a set of car keys.

"What is this, Owen?" Kiana asked him.

"A car," Owen told her enthusiastically. "I know how much you have wanted to replace your old SUV, so I bought you this one a few months ago as a surprise for your birthday."

"I hope you can get your money back," Kiana told him, putting the key back into the box and sliding it to him. "My new position comes with a company pickup truck." That was not a lie, and she was still trying to get used to driving the enormous thing.

"Kiana, this is your car," Owen pushed the box back towards her.

"No, thank you," Kiana ignored the box.

"I want you to come back to me, Kiana," Owen told her. "I want us to live together this time. I want you to be there when I come home in the evenings and to be there for you too when you work late."

"That is very sweet of you," Kiana was a little shocked by what Owen had said.

Owen had always had some excuse or other for the two of them not living together. He hardly even spent an entire night at her apartment, and she only ever slept at his a few times in the two years they had dated.

"Please say you will think about it?" Owen reached for her hand, and she let him take it this time.

"Let me think about it over the weekend," Kiana told him.

"Will you come back to my place for a nightcap?" Owen asked her. "Nothing more. I have another gift for you."

"Owen," Kiana shook her head. "You know that is not a good idea."

"I won't try anything, I promise you," Owen swore to her.

"Fine," Kiana looked at her watch. "I have to make a call quickly. I will meet you outside."

"I will get us a cab," Owen pocketed her present.

"No need," Kiana smiled at him. "I have my company car. It is in the parking garage. I hope your spare parking space is still open?"

"Yes," Owen smiled, letting her go make her phone call while he went to pay the bill.

"You are going where?" Magda asked Kiana with a voice that was full of disdain. "Kiana, I hope you know what you are doing?"

"I will be fine," Kiana assured Magda. "I will be back no later than ten as I still have to pack."

"No need," Magda told her. "I did it as a birthday surprise. Please don't be late and happy birthday. I had a whole thing planned for when you got home."

"Oh, no," Kiana felt awful. "I had forgotten it was my birthday until my father and the kids called."

"You crazy person," Magda laughed. "You have been forgetful lately. That Ronan has warped your brain. If I ever run into him again, I will give him a piece of my mind."

"Mags, he is your boyfriend's sort of brother," Kiana reminded her. "You are bound to run into him. A lot." She warned her friend. "I must go if I am going to get back early."

"Don't drink and drive," Magda told Kiana. "Be safe. Love you."

"No, I won't," Kiana assured Magda. "Will do and love you too." She hung up as Owen walked out of the bar.

"Where is your pickup?" Owen asked her.

"This way," Kiana walked over to a parking lot.

Owen insisted on paying for the parking and looked impressed when he saw the brand-new pickup truck the hotel had given her as her company vehicle.

"Wow," Owen whistled. "It's a beauty."

"I know," Kiana could not help grinning. When she saw it, she immediately thought how much Owen would have loved it. He loved pickup trucks, especially this make and model. "If it were mine, I would let you drive, but only I'm allowed to drive it."

"I understand," Owen grinned. "I am happy to get to drive in it."

Kiana could not help but laugh when he hopped into the passenger seat like a wide-eyed kid in a candy store.

"Can I look now?" Kiana asked Owen, who had his hand covering her eyes while he walked her into his apartment.

"Now you can," Owen pulled his hands away.

Kiana stood amazed, looking around the ultra-modern apartment. It was filled with flowers and happy birthday balloons. The lighting was set to low, with a soft fire crackling in the electric fireplace.

Kiana walked into the apartment, looking around the room. On the dining room table were three different-sized boxes wrapped in bright wrapping paper and gold bows. Next to them was a cake plate with her favorite Oreo, caramel cheesecake, and a champagne bottle on ice.

"You did all this for me?" She asked him in awe.

"Yes," Owen smiled at her. "Of course. I have been planning it for months." He said softly. "That awful day in the office. Renee had been helping me get everything I needed. She found the birthday company to help me decorate while I took you out for a romantic dinner."

Kiana's hand flexed at her side, and she bit her lip, trying not to let the image of that day she had found Renee in Owen's lap make her angry again.

"Thank you, Owen," Kiana turned around, not expecting Owen to be right behind her.

She got such a fright she nearly overbalanced, but Owen reached out and grabbed her. Their eyes met and held while he still had his arms around her. Before Kiana could move, Owen's lips covered hers, and for a moment, she relaxed into the familiar feel of his kiss.

Kiana could not deny that she had wanted Owen to kiss her. She needed to know if she had made a mistake leaving him and if there was still something between them. But as his lips had covered hers, Kiana had known it was not his lips she wanted on hers.

Kiana pulled away from Owen. This was not right, or was it? Ronan did not care. He had some other woman or women for all Kiana knew. Owen was here in front of her. He had bought her a car and done all this for her. Her head spun with confusion.

"Are you okay?" Owen asked her softly, releasing his hold on her a little.

"I'm fine," Kiana said, softly stepping out of his hold. "This is moving a little too fast." She gave him a tight smile.

"I'm sorry," Owen took a step back. He pinched the bridge of his nose. "At least open your presents." He pulled a chair back for her.

"Okay," Kiana shrugged off her coat, which Owen took from her.

"Thank you, Owen," Kiana looked at her watch. She could not believe she had been at Owen's for a little over an hour. "I had a nice time." She smiled at him, her fingers idly playing with the diamond pendant he had given her.

"Will you think about the car?" Owen asked her, hopefully.

"I don't know," Kiana told him honestly. "You have spoiled me so much tonight already." She held up her bag of birthday gifts from him.

Kiana turned to take her coat and then nearly had a heart attack when she turned around to find Owen down on one knee. In his hand, he had a small black velvet box.

"Owen!" Kiana shook her head. Her heart was hammering in her chest.

"Kiana, I love you," Owen's voice was filled with passion. "Will you marry me?"

"Owen," Kiana felt like she had stood up too quickly, and a whooshing noise flooded her ears. Get a grip, Kiana. You are not fainting here! Kiana breathed, steadying herself. "This is too soon."

Owen stood and put the box in her hand.

"Promise me you will think about it over the weekend," Owen reached over to the sideboard and picked up a set of keys on a key ring with her name on it. "These are for you." He handed them to her. "You can come and go when you want. Plus, there is a remote for the parking garage, and my spare parking spot is now yours."

"Oh, Owen," Kiana sighed, stepped forward, and kissed him. "I have to go."

"Promise me you will think about everything over the weekend, and I will let you go," Owen grinned at her holding her captive in his arms.

"Okay," Kiana laughed at him shaking her head. "I promise."

CHAPTER 13
A Wicked Storm

"Oh, no!" Magda looked out the window. "I called the airport, and all flights have been grounded until further notice because of this storm."

"Typical," Kiana stood, staring out of the window. "I decide to get away, and nature grounds me."

"Don't be so down on yourself," Magda told her. "Look on the bright side. We get to stay home and eat all this cake."

"Yes, you're right," Kiana grinned, licking her lips as she eyes out all her favorite desserts.

"Cheesecake for breakfast, then?" Magda shrugged.

"I'm game," Kiana's eyes lit up, and she went to grab spoons. "Dig in."

"Uggghh," Kiana grumbled. "I think we overate the sweet stuff."

"I know, and it is only noon," Magda jumped when the

wind sent a branch slapping against a window. "That tree is going to come right through the glass."

"Let's go out and close the shutters," Kiana suggested.

"Out there?" Magda pointed towards the battle of wind and rain raging outside.

"Yup," Kiana nodded. "If we don't, that tree will invite itself in through a shattering of glass."

"Right!" Magda saw Kiana's point. "Wish we had some warning about this storm."

It was well after four in the afternoon when the storm started to die down. The electricity had gone out a couple of hours ago. Kiana and Magda had started a fire in the living room fireplace, where they had heated a kettle and sat drinking tea, chatting the day away.

"This has been a great day," Kiana told Magda. "I feel relaxed for the first time in days, and I have not felt nauseous once today."

"Wait," Magda frowned at Kiana. "What?"

"I have been feeling run down, tired, and completely drained," Kiana confessed.

"Uh, Kiana," Magda looked at her friend with concern. "Have you been to a doctor about this?"

"No," Kiana shook her head. "I was planning on going on my day off next week. But then I had to change the days around, so I could get this weekend off to go away."

"Good grief, Kiana," Magda shook her head. "You need to go get checked out. If you don't make an appointment with Dr. Thompson tomorrow, I will get Hayden to see you."

"Okay," Kiana held up her hands in surrender. "But I am feeling fine now. I have been stressed out lately. That is all. I probably had an ulcer."

"Uh-huh," Magda said, not convinced. "Tomorrow. We are making you an appointment tomorrow."

Kiana rushed through to the kitchen, where Magda was making coffee.

"Are you going to have something to eat before rushing off?" Magda asked Kiana, concerned. "If you do have an ulcer, you need to eat." She threw Kiana an apple.

"I have to get to work. Poor Simon is taking strain with the damage the storm caused to the hotel," Kiana grabbed her coat and car keys. "I will call Dr. Thompson, I promise." Kiana shook her head, seeing the note Magda had pinned to her coat.

"See that you do," Magda called after Kiana. "Drive safe. Love you."

"Will do," Kiana called over her shoulder. "Love you too."

"I have sorted out a plumber, a carpenter, and an electrician," Kiana told Simon. "They should all be here within an hour."

"Thank goodness for you, Kiana," Simon breathed a sigh of relief. "None of my contacts could get here."

"You need to learn how to use the internet, Simon," Kiana was amazed that Simon battled with the internet. "What thirty-year-old doesn't know how to use the internet?"

"One who prefers books?" Simon grinned at her. "I have never been tech-savvy." He admitted.

"It's okay," Kiana laughed at him. "Your secret is safe with me."

"I know, you are a true gem," Simon stepped into the elevator with Kiana.

"Let's hope the penthouse is not too wrecked," Kiana

crossed her fingers. "It is booked next week by a high-profile client who will not be pleased if he has to be downgraded."

"Oh no," Simon raised his eyebrow. "Please don't tell me it's…"

"I'm afraid so," Kiana nodded. "My second week on the job, and the one guest everyone warned me about is coming to town."

"You make him sound like Santa," Simon laughed, swiping the keycard for the penthouse across the card reader in the elevator.

As the lift bounced to go up, Kiana was overcome with a giddy spell. She felt like she could not breathe, and all the oxygen was being sucked from her lungs. Her face turned ashen as Kiana turned to look at Simon, who looked stricken. She could see his lips moving but could not hear what he was saying.

"Kiana," Simon's voice penetrated the black void that had dragged Kiana down.

Her eyes opened and focused on a panicked-looking Simon.

"Are you with me?" Simon dabbed an ice-cold towel on her face.

"What happened?" Kiana tried to sit up, but the world tilted.

"Not sure, but you went grey, then flopped to the floor," Simon told her.

"Where are we?" She looked around, and her mouth felt dry. "Is there some water?"

"Yes," Simon reached over and gave her an icy cold bottle of water. "We are in the penthouse suite."

"I'm so sorry," Kiana sipped the water, and her stomach

rolled. She forced herself to sit up. "I have been feeling a little under the weather lately."

"Honey, you have been working yourself around the clock here," Simon told her. "I know you are new and want to take in everything, but you must slow down. I don't want to lose you."

"Thank you," Kiana smiled at him. "So, how's the suite looking?"

"I don't see any damage," Simon took stock. "All three bedrooms are still intact, but the hot water is out, and a few bulbs have blown."

"I will get them replaced and let the plumber know about the hot water," Kiana took a deep breath and stood up slowly.

"You, young lady, will do nothing of the sort," Simon informed her, handing her a piece of paper with a time on it. "Your friend, Magda, gave me strict instructions to get you an appointment with one Dr. Thompson, which Lindsey from the front desk so kindly did for you."

"I was going to do that later today," Kiana told him, her cheeks flaming with embarrassment.

"Come now, Kiana," Simon looked at her. "I told you we are family here in this establishment. The owner insists his staff members are well taken care of."

"That is very kind, but I am fine now," Kiana tried to assure him.

"Your appointment is in an hour," Simon looked at his watch pointedly. "You have a lot of traffic to get through in this mess. So off with you and don't come back until you are better, and that is an order." Simon pushed her into the elevator.

Needles freaked Kiana out, and so did the sight of blood. She sat feeling sorry for herself and poked the Band-Aid covering the little hole from having drawn blood had made.

Where was the doctor? Kiana fidgeted. She wanted to get her medication and go. Not that she would take the medicine, but it seemed to make the doctors and everyone around her feel better. Kiana preferred the good old-fashioned-suffering-through-the-pain method to putting junk in her system.

"Kiana," Dr. Thompson stepped into the examination room with Kiana's chart in her hands. "As I expected, it is not an ulcer."

"I thought you needed to do a scan or scope thingy to find that out?" Kiana frowned at the doctor.

"To be honest, Kiana, I was not checking for an ulcer," Dr. Thompson's brows drew together. "Kiana, I was testing to see if you were pregnant because that is what your symptoms implied."

"What?" Kiana choked. "I don't understand?" Her mind reeled, immediately rejecting the idea.

"I'm afraid it's true, Kiana," Dr. Thompson confirmed. "What I would like to do is an ultrasound if that is okay with you?"

"I ..." Kiana looked at the doctor, confused. "No," Kiana gave a little laugh. "Surely not!"

A ringing started in Kiana's ears as the implications of what the doctor had said sunk in. Kiana immediately knew who the father was, which did not sit well with her.

"Kiana?" Dr. Thompson looked at her, concerned. "Are you okay? Do you want me to call someone for you?"

"No," Kiana shook her head. "Do you mind if I do the ..." Kiana could not think of the word.

"Ultrasound," Dr. Thompson filled in for her.

"Another time," Kiana gave the doctor a tight smile. "I have to go."

"Kiana," Dr. Thompson scribbled out two notes. "These are some vitamins you should take, and this is a sick note. You are a bit dehydrated, and you need some rest, so I have booked you off work for five days."

"Thank you," Kiana stood up, taking the notes.

"I need to see you again in five days," the doctor told her. "I will get my front desk to make the appointment and message you."

Kiana nodded, not paying much attention to what the doctor had said. Her mind was reeling. She wanted to go home, curl into a little ball, pull her blanket over her head, and just hide away for the rest of her life.

CHAPTER 14
Hiding Away From the World

"Poor baby," Magda brought Kiana a bowl of warm soup and some toast. "You stay curled up in bed. I won't be home too late, but Hayden wants to tell me something."

"You go," Kiana smiled at Magda. "I'm just going to cuddle up on the sofa and watch a movie."

"Okay," Magda fussed around Kiana. "Let's get you settled there, then."

"Mags, I'm fine; go have fun with your guy," Kiana smiled weakly at her friend, feeling guilty for not having the courage to tell her the truth about her pregnancy. Instead, she had told Magda what she had told everyone else. She had stomach flu.

Kiana's good friend William, a pharmacist, had given her some placebo tablets to make it seem she was taking medication. He had also given her some aspirin for a pregnant friend who had a headache. Kiana may not have accepted her circumstance yet or could not bring herself to believe it, but that did not mean she wanted to cause it harm. However, she did have a splitting headache, and the doctor had said she could take the tablets William had got for her.

"Okay," Magda hugged Kiana. "Get some rest. I will be back in a few hours."

"Have fun," Kiana smiled at Magda.

Kiana must have dozed off as she nearly fell off the couch with fright when the front door opened.

"I'm sorry," Magda whispered. "I didn't mean to wake you." She tiptoed up to Kiana with her hand behind her back.

"What's going on?" Kiana eyed Magda suspiciously.

"Hayden asked me to marry him," Magda could not help it; her excitement burst out. She put her hand out to show Kiana her large square-cut diamond ring.

"Oh, wow!" tears sprung to Kiana's eyes. She could not help it. A wave of emotions swelled up inside of her and swooshed down on her. "I am so happy for you." Before she could stop them, the waterworks broke, and Kiana started to sob.

"Oh, Kiana," Magda sat down next to her friend, alarmed. "I'm sorry; I didn't mean to upset you."

"It's not you," Kiana sniffled. "I am so thrilled for you. You deserve this. Hayden is the best." Kiana wailed.

"I don't understand why you are ...." Magda's eyes fell on the prescription from Dr. Thompson. "Wait a minute. Kiana, are you pregnant?"

Kiana's eyes flew to her friend in fright before she burst into tears all over again.

"I'm sorry," Kiana hiccupped. The tears had finally subsided. "I wasn't lying to you. I was still in denial about it myself."

"I understand, Kiana," Magda soothed. "To be honest, I had suspected it a while ago."

"Why didn't you say anything?" Kiana dabbed at her swollen eyes.

"Because you had enough emotional baggage to carry around," Magda smiled at her. "Now, drink your peppermint tea."

"Yes, mom," Kiana gave Magda a watery smile. It felt so good to have gotten all that off her chest. "So, when will you get married, or will this be a long engagement?"

"Well," Magda looked at Kiana oddly. "That is another thing Hayden needed to discuss with me."

"Okay …" Kiana's eyes narrowed as she looked at Magda.

"Hayden has got this once-in-a-lifetime opportunity to go study these new techniques in Switzerland," Magda fiddled nervously with her fingers. "He does not want to leave me behind, so he wants to get married before he leaves."

"When does he leave?" Kiana asked, not liking where this was going.

"In three weeks," Magda said quickly and then gave a toothy grin.

"Three weeks!" Kiana spat. "What kind of wedding, big or small?"

"His uncle has offered to host it at his estate for us," Magda told her. "It will only be close family and friends. As Hayden and I don't have much family, there will be no more than ten to fifteen people there."

"Okay," Kiana was instantly on high alert about going to the Waters estate. "I guess this means Ronan will be there."

"That is the other thing," Magda said. "I want you to be my maid of honor, and Ronan is going to be his best man." She pulled a face.

"I will do this for you," Kiana told her. "Of course, you

know that. But you have to promise that my condition stays between us until I decide what to do.

"Kiana, you know I would never say a thing," Magda looked quite offended by that.

"I know," Kiana hugged her friend. "I just needed to make sure."

"One more thing," Magda said. "I need someone to look after my house and boutique while I am gone. Now, I am not asking you to run it; Chloe can do that. But I will need you to oversee it, and I would like you to take care of my house."

"Of course," Kiana told Magda.

"I need you to start this week because we are flying to Switzerland for a few days tomorrow to find a house." Magda grinned.

"Oh, my word!" Kiana could not believe her friend's good fortune. "I am so happy for you."

"I feel so bad leaving you in this state," Magda told her.

"Don't you dare feel bad about being so happy," Kiana said. "I will be fine; besides, this is something I have to figure out for myself."

The house was so empty without Magda, Kiana thought, putting on some water for her morning ginger tea. It tasted horrible, but it helped with nausea. Kiana had an hour before she had to go to the boutique to make peace with Chloe. She was not looking forward to that.

But if they were going to be working together, Kiana had to apologize to her and clear the air. Chloe was about to take her first sip of the dreaded ginger tea when the doorbell rang. She was not expecting anyone.

"Owen?" Kiana looked up at him, shocked. "What are you doing here?"

"I called your work as you were not answering my calls, and they told me you were sick," Owen looked at her worriedly.

"I'm fine, just stressed with a bit of stomach flu." Was that even a thing? Kiana thought.

"You should have told me your flight was grounded and you were stuck here for the weekend," Owen looked down at her. "I could have come over."

"I thought you were giving me the weekend to think things over?" Kiana told him, folding her arms defensively across her body.

"I'm sorry," Owen held up his hand. "I'm doing it again, aren't I?"

"It's okay," Kiana shrugged. "I'm fine, Owen. Thank you for stopping by, but I have an appointment I have to get to."

"Of course," Owen gave her a small smile. "I stopped by the boutique, and that young woman told me Magda was out of town for a while."

"So?" Kiana looked at him questioningly.

"You shouldn't be on your right now," Owen told her worriedly. "Why not come stay at my place, at least for a night or two? I promise you can have your own room, and I won't put any pressure on you."

"I'm fine right here, Owen," Kiana told him. "But I will come for dinner tonight; how about that?"

Why not? Kiana thought. Magda was getting married and then moving to Switzerland for a year. Kiana would be all alone, so why not give Owen another chance?

"Really?" Owen asked enthusiastically. "I will get all your favorite foods."

"Just a green salad and club soda for me," Kiana said. "My stomach is very sensitive."

"Of course," Owen shook his head. "I will see you at six?"

"Six it is," Kiana nodded before stepping inside and closing the front door.

What was she doing? Kiana breathed deeply, leaning against the door.

Kiana was surprised at how much she was enjoying the evening with Owen. He was sweet, kind, and sensitive to her being ill. He had even taken the following day off work to be with her and make sure she was alright.

"Would you like to watch a movie?" Owen asked, looking at his watch. "It is still quite early."

"Sure," Kiana smiled at Owen. "Why not? What did you have in mind?"

"I wanted to watch this new action movie," Owen sat down next to Kiana on the sofa as he flipped through the movies. "Here it is."

Shock zinged through Kiana. It was the same movie she and Ronan had watched that weekend she had stayed at his place.

"Kiana?" Owen asked, concerned. "Are you okay?"

"Yes," Kiana gave Owen a tight smile. "Let's watch."

Owen smiled back, clicked play on the move, and then pulled a blanket over them to keep them cozy while they watched.

Kiana felt like she was floating. She opened her heavy eyelids to find herself in Owen's arms, being carried into his spare bedroom.

"Owen?" Kiana looked at him sleepily. "What time is it?"

"Late," Owen smiled at her softly. "We both fell asleep during the movie." He looked apologetic.

"Okay," Kiana yawned, letting Owen slip off her shoes and tuck her into bed.

"Sleep tight, Kiana," Owen said, kissing her forehead.

"Owen," Kiana snuggled into the pillow.

"Yes?" Owen stared down at her.

"Will you stay with me tonight?" Kiana's eyes started to close. "I don't want to be alone."

"Of course," Owen smiled. He pulled off his shoes and climbed in on the other side of the bed.

Kiana turned over and cuddled onto his chest. She sighed, feeling his strong arms circle her and pull her closer.

CHAPTER 15
Welcome Home, Magda

Kiana's sick days had flown by, and Simon had insisted on changing her weekend shift so she could have another two days off. Magda was due back from her trip to Switzerland the next day, and they had a lot of planning to do. Kiana was so excited to see the wedding dress Magda had bought on her trip.

Kiana still could not believe Magda was getting married again and so soon. She could understand the need for a small wedding, though. Magda had already had her fairytale one. Bless Todd for that, Kiana thought. She was so glad Magda had found her second true love.

"Morning, Kiana," Lindsey greeted Kiana cheerfully as she walked into the lobby.

"Morning, Lindsey," Kiana smiled at the young woman. "Is there anything I need to know or fires that need putting out before I get started on the fourth-floor renovations?"

"Yes," Lindsey nodded, looking serious. "Simon said to tell you I was to get you to the dining room as soon as you got in. Something about something you forgot?" She shrugged.

"What?" Kiana felt a little alarmed. Her memory had not been that good lately. What had she forgotten?

"Come on then," Lindsey led the way, fiddling with her phone as they walked.

"You should not walk and text," Kiana warned her.

"What?" Lindsey lifted her head. "Oh, yeah. I know." She nodded and then grinned before dramatically swinging the dining room doors open.

The staff yelled happy birthday, nearly giving Kiana a heart attack before a lump swelled up in her throat.

"We are sorry it is a bit late," Simon walked up to her and handed her an orange juice. "But it seems someone forgot to mention it was her special day before she got sick."

Tears sparkled in Kiana's eyes.

"Simon, this is so sweet," Kiana greeted everyone and thanked them before digging into her favorite Oreo caramel cheesecake.

"What time is that conference wrapping up?" Kiana looked at her wristwatch. "I have the shipping company coming in three hours for their CEO's birthday, and the staff still has to decorate."

"I think they are wrapping up now," Lindsey informed Kiana. Just that morning, Lindsey shared with Kiana that she had been promoted and was now her assistant. "I asked the two serving staff for an update."

"I am so glad Simon appointed you as my assistant," Kiana smiled at the young woman. "We have only worked together for nearly a day, and already you know how to read my mind."

"I begged him," Lindsey told her honestly. "Then, when he did not listen, I kept at him the entire week until he finally caved in."

"A girl after my own heart," Kiana looked at Lindsey, impressed. "That sounds like something I would have done at your age."

Lindsey grinned at Kiana.

"Can you go find out where the heck the next lot of designers are?" Kiana asked Lindsey. "They were supposed to be here an hour ago."

"Sure thing," Lindsey was about to step away before returning to Kiana. "Would you like another ginger tea?"

"Please; anything but that?" Kiana rolled her eyes.

"How about a peppermint Oreo caffeine-free latte?" Lindsey asked.

"That would be awesome," Kiana sighed. "I think I love you." She said exaggeratedly.

Lindsey rolled her eyes before rushing off. Kiana had no choice but to tell Simon and then Lindsey about her pregnancy. They had both been so excited for her; Kiana had felt overwhelmed. She was not used to having such supportive and caring work people around her. They had also agreed not to let anyone else know until Kiana had decided what to do about her situation.

Kiana's phone bleeped to inform her she had received a message. She looked down to find it was from Owen. A smile spread across Kiana's face. It was an invitation in the shape of a heart to join him for dinner tonight at his place. After their dinner and movie night, Kiana had spent most of her sick week off with Owen at his apartment.

They had not made love but had kissed and cuddled. Owen had been a perfect gentleman on the nights she had stayed over and just laid with her, holding her through the night. She knew he was waiting for her answer about getting married and moving in with him. He had mentioned only twice, bringing up Magda's wedding and the fact she was moving to Switzerland. He had even suggested maybe they both moved into Magda's house until they could find their own.

It had been three weeks since Kiana had last seen Ronan. She knew he had asked Hayden about her because Magda had told her every time Hayden mentioned it to her. Kiana had given Magda permission to tell Hayden why Kiana had taken off, and he had been furious with his friend. But Magda had made him swear not to say nothing to Ronan and let it be. What a great guy Hayden was when you got behind those high walls he had up around him.

Kiana was distracted when Magda's message came. They were coming home early and moving the wedding up to Saturday. As there were only a handful of people, and most of the preparation was already done by Bruce's staff, they decided not to wait.

Kiana toyed with her phone. Her heart was skipping a little, thinking that a week was not enough time for her to be ready to see Ronan again. She was not looking where she was going and collided with another woman walking out of a guest bathroom.

The woman dropped her phone. Kiana started apologizing, bending down to pick up the phone, freezing as a familiar deep voice called to the woman.

"Valerie, are you okay?" Ronan rushed over to where the two women had collided.

Kiana wished she could crawl into the cabinet next to her and hideaway.

"I'm fine, thank you, Ronan," Kiana heard the woman all but purr.

"Kiana?" Ronan bent down to where she was crouched on the floor.

"Hello, Ronan," Kiana swallowed, trying to still her traitorous heart.

"I ..." Ronan's eyes devoured her as he stood staring.

"Ronan, we need to get going," the woman Kiana had bumped into said impatiently.

Kiana turned to look at the woman and froze. She was the woman who had sent Ronan those messages that day. She would recognize those pouty lips and perfectly groomed blond locks in an instant. The woman's face had burned into her memory. Now she was standing there looking at Kiana like a speck of dirt on her expensive shoes.

"Go get the valet to bring the car around," Ronan handed the woman the ticket. "I will be there in a minute."

The woman looked taken aback before glaring at Kiana and then storming off.

"I have to go," Kiana tried to step around Ronan, but he grabbed her arms and wouldn't let her. "Please let go of me."

"No," Ronan breathed. "I have been trying to get hold of you for three weeks, Kiana." He sounded anxious. "Please tell me why you ran away and never looked back. I thought we were moving our relationship forward. I thought you felt the same way about me." He shook his head. "No, I know you felt the same way about me as I do about you."

"Why don't you ask Valerie over there?" Kiana's eyes were stormy when they met Ronan's. "I heard your phone ring. It was between the seats of your car. It stopped ringing by the time I found it, but there were a lot of messages about missing your hot, warm body next to hers." She forcefully knocked his hands from her arms.

"What?" Ronan looked at her, confused. "Valerie and I have been over for months. We are business colleagues looking to take over this small hotel chain."

"Good for you," Kiana told him sarcastically. "Now, if you don't mind, I have to go to meet my father. He is staying here, and I am late to join him for an early dinner in the penthouse." She lied. She could not get the image of the way Valerie had looked at her 0ut of her head.

"Your father is here?" Ronan gave her a sad smile. "That is great."

"Thank you," Kiana tried to step past him once again, but he stopped her.

"Kiana," Ronan said softly. "There was nothing between Valerie and me from the moment I scooped you up off the gym floor." He sighed. "I love you. I have been beside myself trying to get hold of you."

"It's too late for that, Ronan," Kiana told him. "Owen and I are engaged."

Ronan's face paled, his shoulder stiffened, and his eyes went dull as he stared into Kiana's eyes for a few seconds before nodding.

"You know he is not the man you were meant to marry," Ronan told her softly before stepping past her. "When you realize that, you know where to find me." He gave her a soft kiss on the top of her head before walking away.

Kiana stood, breathing deeply. Her legs felt like jelly, and her stomach rolled. She rushed into the bathroom and collapsed on top of one of the toilet seats after locking the door. She sat there, holding her stomach and willing the tears away.

Kiana was determined not to cry. Slowly the shakiness subsided, and she began to be in control of her senses once again. At least the shock of seeing him again was over. That would make it a tiny bit less awkward for her on Saturday.

CHAPTER 16
A Beautiful Wedding

The rest of the week seemed to fly by. Magda had arrived home in a flurry of excitement and last-minute wedding preparation. She had decided she wanted a girl's night in with Kiana and Chloe for her last night as a single lady on Friday night. Chloe and Kiana had obliged her by giving her a home spa night.

Saturday came around too soon. Kiana drove Magda and Chloe to the Waters' house in the countryside while Paul, Chloe's boyfriend, followed behind them with Owen. On the drive to Ronan's family home, all Kiana could think of was that meeting with him on Monday. It had played through her mind over and over again in a flurry of emotions. Kiana was all tangled up in guilt, confusion, and a whole lot of hurt mixed with a good dose of boiling anger.

But today was not the day to let her messed up life get in the way of her best friend's big day. Today, Kiana would focus on Magda and getting through this day. In a couple of hours, they would be on their way home, and she would not have to think of Ronan ever again.

Kiana had already half made up her mind to accept

Owen's proposal. She knew they had to have a serious conversation first, though. Kiana touched her stomach. She could no longer deny its presence in her life and had scheduled another appointment with Dr. Thompson for the following week. Kiana had wanted to tell her family before discussing it with Owen.

"Are you ready for this?" Chloe asked Kiana worriedly.

When Magda had been away, Chloe and Kiana had become quite close. She had become Kiana's Magda stand-in, and Kiana had become Chloe's. Chloe now knew everything, including what a big liar Kiana had been to Ronan.

"I think so," Kiana whispered to Chloe, giving her a grateful smile. "Thank you."

"I'm here if you need anything," Chloe assured Kiana softly, stiffening when she saw the red sports car zooming up the drive. "I presume that is the playboy?" she drawled.

"Yes," Magda popped over their shoulder as they piled out of Kiana's pickup truck. "And I take it that the blonde is who we now know to be Valerie." Magda's eyes narrowed in on the woman.

"Hi, ladies," Ronan pulled two bags from the trunk of his car as he called to them. "Nice pickup." He walked over to eye it out.

Kiana was so grateful that the hotel had not yet gotten the banners put on it.

"It was a present from Kiana's father for her birthday a few weeks ago," Chloe told Ronan, stepping forward with her hand held out. "I'm Chloe, bridesmaid and best friend number two."

"Ronan," Ronan shook Chloe's hand.

"I know!" Chloe pulled her hand away, then, ignoring the blonde, turned to help Magda and Kiana with the bags.

"Can I help you ladies with anything?" Ronan stepped

around the truck, his eyes meeting Kiana's. "Hi," he smiled at her as if she was mesmerizing.

"Ronan," Kiana said abruptly while Magda completely ignored him to turn and greet the family bustling out the front door of the manor.

"Here," Ronan dropped his bags to reach for the box Kiana was pulling from the car.

"That's okay," Owen's voice came from behind them. "I've got it." He smiled at Ronan.

"Thanks, Owen," Kiana smiled at Owen, giving him the box.

"Sorry, I'm Owen," Owen held out his hand to Ronan from beneath the box.

"Ronan," Ronan eyed the man out, realizing he knew nothing about him and Kiana.

"Shall we?" Chloe grabbed Paul's arm and dragged him away before any more introductions were made.

"Thank you," Kiana said softly to Chloe.

"You're so welcome," Chloe hugged Kiana. "Did you see how that woman looked at us all?"

"Like we were dirt on expensive shoes?" Kiana managed a grin.

"Yes," Chloe's brows drew together. "She is nothing but a bimbo, yet thinks she can look down on us when she knows nothing about us," she said indignantly.

Even though Valerie clung to Ronan's arm like a vine, the day was beautiful. Chloe had come to Kiana's rescue before she crumbled into an emotional wreck a few times during the day.

As the wedding started to wind down, Kiana knew they should be returning to the city, but she could not help but wish this was her wedding day. It had been a perfect small but elaborated wedding, one that she had always dreamed of having.

Kiana's eyes fell on Owen, who was dancing with Chloe. She smiled, knowing in her heart that it was not hers and Owen's wedding she wanted this to be. As if reading her mind, the man she had managed to avoid the entire day stepped up behind her.

"It felt right having you on my arm walking down the aisle," Ronan was so close behind her she could feel the heat of his body as his breath tickled her back.

"I could not wait for us to part," Kiana told him coldly, referring to their awkward walk up the aisle as the maid of honor and best man.

"Liar," Ronan laughed softly. "Do you think I cannot see the way that little pulse in your neck starts to beat when we get too close?" He put his finger on it. "That is exactly what mine does too."

Kiana closed her eyes, gathering her strength. Ronan was here with that woman who had sent him those texts. She was more convinced than ever that they had been together at the same time she and Ronan were.

"I think your girlfriend is looking for you," Kiana pointed to Valerie, who was scanning the guests.

"She is not my girlfriend," Ronan hissed in her ear. "If you would stop for one minute and hear me out, you would know that."

"Please, Ronan," Kiana suddenly felt exhausted. "I can't do this now. It is my friend's day, and I am tired." She put her empty club soda glass in his hand and turned to go.

"He is not the man for you, Kiana," Ronan said as she walked away.

"Thank you so much for coming with me, Chloe," Kiana held Chloe's hand nervously as they waited for Dr. Thompson.

"I would not miss this for the world," Chloe told Kiana. "Thank you for asking me to be with you."

Magda had left for Switzerland, and Kiana was so glad she still had Chloe. Earlier, Kiana had gotten a surprise call from Chloe's boyfriend, Paul. He asked her to help him determine what kind of ring Chloe would want as an engagement ring. It seemed everyone around Kiana had the wedding bug. That is why she had decided she would visit her family this weekend. Kiana could finally tell Owen; she would accept his proposal if he still wanted to marry her.

"Kiana," Chloe said seriously. "Are you going to tell the father of the child?"

"Yes," Kiana told Chloe honestly. "I am going to tell my family first this weekend."

"Are you sure you don't want me to accompany you?" Chloe asked.

"This is something I have to do on my own," Kiana smiled gratefully at Chloe. "It is time I grew up."

"I think you are doing an amazing job of coping," Chloe told Kiana.

"Hello, ladies," Dr. Thompson stepped into the room. "Are we ready to take a look at the little person?"

CHAPTER 17
Life on a Repeating Loop

"I will call you when I get there," Kiana assured Chloe. "I promise if my father threatens to kill me, to call you right away."

Kiana grinned at how overly protective Chloe had become since they had seen the ultrasound. Chloe had insisted she shares joint guardianship of the baby with Magda.

"I see Chloe has stepped in as the new Magda," Owen's voice held a hint of disapproval. "Just when I thought I would finally have you all to myself." He leaned down and grabbed her for a passionate kiss.

"I need my friends too, Owen," Kiana gave Owen a tight smile. "Now I must go, or I will be late for my flight."

"Are you sure I cannot drive you to the airport?" Owen asked her while putting her suitcase in the back of Kiana's pickup truck.

"No," Kiana smiled at him. "This way, if I do get the early flight back, I don't have to worry about you coming to fetch me."

"Fetching you is only a pleasure," Owen kissed her before closing the car door.

"Thank you," Kiana gave him a peck on the cheek. "I will see you in three days."

"Have a good time," Owen stepped aside, waving to her as she pulled out of Magda's driveway.

"The flight has been delayed!" Kiana said to her father in frustration.

"Okay, honey, let us know when you have more details," Kiana's father told her from the other side of the phone. "Go sit and have one of those weird latte coffee things you like so much."

"I think I might do that," Kiana grinned. Since she had the heart-to-heart talk about losing her previous job with her dad, their relationship had improved.

Kiana walked into the coffee and ordered her latte. As she sat down to drink it, her eyes caught the cover of a magazine. The title read, Will Ronan Waters finally be settling down? Shock spread through her system as Ronan, being kissed by Valerie on some beach, sprung out at her. The now-familiar anger shot through her, and pain ripped through her heart. Why should she care? She had decided to accept Owen's proposal after the weekend!

Not wanting to see the picture that slapped in her face, Kiana left her half-drunk latte and headed for the waiting lounge. When she was halfway to the gate, it was announced that her flight had been canceled due to engine trouble with the plane.

She stopped, and a thought struck her. Maybe it was fate telling her that there was no time like the present to accept

Owen's proposal. Besides, she had been carrying his ring in her purse ever since he had proposed. The announcement told all passengers to collect their luggage and get a refund or check in for the next flight.

Kiana did not care about that right now. She was going to surprise Owen. Kiana was going to tell him everything. Excitement coursed through her as she quickly rolled her carry-on through the airport. Kiana finally had a job she loved, a new best friend, and a happy, life-long best friend. Kiana had a lovely house, and now she would mend her relationship status.

Kiana aimed the remote control at the parking garage's door and giggled. She had no idea why the simple process of the door sliding open, granting her access, made her feel so important, but it did. She felt like she mattered enough to have her own parking space in her boyfriend's apartment block. It even felt good to be calling Owen her boyfriend again.

A feeling of dread clawed its way through her at what she had to confess to Owen. But these past weeks had proven him to be so understanding and in love with her that Kiana was sure he would forgive her.

Kiana frowned when she noticed a small white sports car parked in her space. She even doubled to check to make sure it was her space. Kiana would have to tell Owen about this. She parked a few parking spaces down in a bay she knew was not occupied.

The ride up to his apartment floor had Kiana wholly tied up in knots about how she would start the conversation. When Kiana let herself into his apartment, she felt so nervous that she worried she would throw up. When Kiana put her keys on the hook, there was a strange set of keys hanging there.

Kiana's brows drew together as she looked at the jeweled S of the key ring.

Kiana turned to find Owen when she heard noises coming from his bedroom. A cold feeling swept over Kiana as a sense of déjà vu hit her. The sounds of passion got louder when Kiana stood outside Owen's bedroom door. Kiana had a sick feeling that the diamond-studded S key ring stood for Renee. Her suspicions were proved correct when she pushed the door open and found a naked Renee straddling an equally naked Owen.

Kiana stood there, staring blankly at them for a few minutes before slamming the door shut. Kiana fiddled in her purse, pulling out the blue velvet box, which she dumped on the side table as she grabbed her coat and keys before storming out of the apartment.

Kiana heard Owen shouting after her as the lift doors slid shut and zoomed her down to the basement. She also knew whose little white car was parked in her parking bay. Tears streamed down her face as Kiana pulled out of the parking bay. She could not believe this had happened to her again. It was now clear that she was not meant for a happily ever after when it came to romance.

"Well, baby," Kiana whispered to the little person growing inside her. "It is going to be you and me against the world. How does that sound?"

She dialed Chloe's number, but there was no answer, and Hanna's phone went to voicemail. Kiana sobbed a message of what had happened to Chloe's answering service. When she hung up, Kiana found herself heading toward the coast. Kiana did not care. She just needed to drive. Kiana's love life seemed to play on a repeated life loop of one cheating relationship after the other.

Kiana was so distraught and her eyes blurry with tears that

she did not have time to react when the motorist in front of her swerved to miss a deer, skidded, and suddenly stopped. The deer jumped away, but Kiana braked too late and hit the stopped vehicle. The last thing she remembered was being glad the deer was okay.

CHAPTER 18
The Hospital

Ronan rushed into the hospital. He could not believe the phone call he had gotten. The nurses at the front desk took him through to where he needed to be. There, the doctor told him that the driver had been fortunate and had only sustained a broken leg. Ronan sighed with relief.

The doctor gave Ronan twenty minutes to see the patient.

"Hey there," Ronan walked into the hospital room. "Look at you all banged up."

"I know, right!" Marcus, Ronan's long-time assistant, tried to grin. But his eyes looked sleepy. "So sorry about this. A deer jumped into the road on my way to the Parker estate. I lost control of the vehicle trying to avoid it, and this pickup truck T-boned me."

"How is the other driver?" Ronan asked.

"I'm not sure," Marcus said, his tired eyes filled with worry. "I hope I did not kill them."

"Stop that," Ronan told Marcus. "None of this is your fault."

"I should have been paying more attention," Marcus told Ronan.

"You concentrate on getting better," Ronan told Marcus. "I will go and see the other driver."

"Thank you, Ronan," Marcus started to drift off to sleep. "You are a prince."

Ronan watched Marcus drift off. From what the rescue workers had told Ronan, they had to cut the other passenger out of their car with the Jaws of Life. A chill crept up his spine. He hoped the other driver was going to be okay.

Ronan left Marcus to go and find a doctor to ask about the driver of the other vehicle. One of his company cars on company business had caused the accident. Ronan would take full responsibility for it. That included covering all medical expenses and any vehicle repairs or replacement costs. Ronan stopped for a minute and breathed. That is if the other driver was in recovery. He refused to think about that.

Be positive, Ronan! But lately, Ronan has not been optimistic about too much. He felt bruised. Ronan never went anywhere anymore except to work and family functions. Besides that, he spent most of his time cooped up in his apartment when he was not at the office or gym.

Ronan found the doctor that had attended to Marcus.

"I know this is not policy," Ronan told the doctor, "but would it be possible to speak to the other driver involved in my assistant's accident?" He explained his plans to the doctor.

"The lady's family has been informed, but they cannot get here for a few days," the doctor walked Ronan to another part of the hospital. "Her friend is with her now, but you will not be able to talk to her without her friend's or family's consent."

"Could you not ask the driver?" Ronan looked at the doctor, a little confused and alarmed, thinking it had been a minor driving the car.

"The other driver is in a coma, I'm afraid," the doctor

informed Ronan. "She is currently unable to give consent. But her family assured me her friend could do so on her behalf until they arrive."

"I see," Ronan nodded as they stopped outside the room.

"I will go call Miss Davies," the doctor gave Ronan a tight smile and walked into the room.

Ronan knew he should not be rude, but he couldn't help taking a peek through the glass window where the blind was not pulled fully closed. His heart stopped in his chest when he realized who Miss Davies was. Ronan had met her before at Magda's wedding. Her name was Chloe, if he remembered correctly. His breath caught in his throat, and his mind reeled as a feeling of dread crept over him.

Surely not! Ronan thought. Part of him wanted to turn and run and deny it. Part of him wanted to run into the room and hold her to him, begging her to wake up. But he stood frozen on the spot as the doctor stepped aside, and he saw her beautiful face.

"Kiana!" Ronan breathed and rushed into the room before he could stop himself.

"What is he doing here?" Chloe hissed at the doctor.

"This is the gentleman who would like to talk to you. The other driver's boss!" The doctor looked at them both.

"You know her?" The doctor pointed to Kiana, not Chloe.

"She's the woman I love," Ronan said softly, ignoring Chloe and the doctor. He walked over to the bed where Kiana laid lifeless with a tube feeding her oxygen.

"I'm sorry, Mr. Waters," the doctor moved to call security.

"It's okay," Chloe smiled at the doctor.

"Are you sure?" The doctor asked her before leaving the room.

"How bad is she?" Ronan's voice was gravelly. His eyes lifted to look at Chloe. They were filled with tears.

"The doctors will know more in the morning," Chloe wanted to fling him out of the room. But she knew real grief and heartache when she saw it. And Ronan was a man currently in shock and pain.

Ronan put one hand on Hanna's head and the other over her cold one resting on her stomach. He dropped his head onto the pillow next to Kiana's.

"Please, Kiana, come back to me," Ronan whispered as the tears spilled over his lids and rolled down his cheeks.

"Sit," Chloe pulled up a chair for him. "When you have calmed down, we can have a nice chat."

It had been the longest two days of Ronan's life. After a rocky start, he and Chloe started to get along. He could see she was still wary of him and a bit tight-lipped about the information on this Owen guy Kiana was engaged to. However, Ronan was yet to see the man at the hospital.

"It is not my place to tell you about Owen," Chloe told Ronan for the fourth time. "But if you happened to go through my phone, I just happened to leave here while I got us a coffee," she put the phone on the table at the door of Kiana's hospital room, "that would not be my fault."

Ronan smiled as Chloe left the room to pursue some coffee, although he now knew Chloe did not drink either tea or coffee. He felt a bit sleazy going through Chloe's phone, but he needed to know. Ronan found the message and was nearing the end when he saw Kiana's eyes trying to open. The anger he had felt at the message Kiana had left about catching Owen with another woman quickly faded at the sight of Kiana waking up.

Ronan jumped up and rushed to find a nurse or a doctor.

"You let Ronan listen to your message?" Kiana accused Chloe.

"Yeah," Chloe nodded, not feeling a bit of guilt. "You should have seen the guy. He was an emotional wreck. And we talked the whole night right here by your bedside."

"Great," Kiana sighed, then winced.

"You need to talk to him, Kiana," Chloe said gently. "He does love you, and he let me go through his phone. I am talking about months of messages."

"You went through his phone?" Kiana shook her head.

"Of course," Chloe's brows drew together. "It is a matter of trust."

"I thought not going through someone's phone was a matter of trust," Kiana rolled her eyes at Chloe.

"Nope," Chloe contradicted her. "If you have nothing to hide, it should not matter if you go through each other's phones. And your father sends his love and is glad you are okay," Chloe told her. "He is sorry they cannot get here, but Tammy had to return for her second round of treatment."

"I understand," Kiana smiled. Her head and ribs ached. Her hands went to her stomach.

"Little one is okay too," Chloe said, amazed. "Apparently, he was a lot safer than you were."

"He?" Kiana looked at Chloe curiously.

"Yeah," Chloe nodded. "That's my guess for my little boy." She winked at Kiana.

"Who knows?" Kiana looked at Chloe in shock.

"Who knows what?" Ronan popped his head in the door, holding a bunch of red roses.

Kiana looked from him to Chloe, who gave her a reassuring smile and shook her head, confirming Ronan was none the wiser.

Kiana looked relieved before her bruised eyes met him.

"I am so glad to see you awake," Ronan told her softly.

"I am going to get coffee," Chloe took her wallet from her purse. "I am also hungry. I will be back in about twenty minutes." She looked directly at Ronan before leaving the room.

CHAPTER 19
The Patient

Kiana could not believe she had let her friend bully her into accepting Ronan's offer of recovering at his new house on the beach. Granted, it was a beautiful house with an incredible view of being right on the beach. But it meant seeing him daily, and Kiana's stomach started looking a little bulgy.

"Kiana?" Ronan called her. "Are you okay? May I come in?" He creaked her bedroom door and opened it a crack.

"Sure," Kiana said resignedly.

"The nurse told me you are still refusing the pain medication the doctor prescribed you," Ronan walked onto the balcony, where he found her once again staring out at sea.

"It is pretty here," Kiana told him, not bothering to look up at him.

"I thought of you when I bought it," Ronan's voice dropped as he leaned against the railing, looking out over the ocean.

"Thank you for the water," Kiana said and stood up, wincing as her ribs objected to the sudden movement.

"Careful," Ronan spun around, reaching out to help her, only to have her swat him away.

"I can manage on my own," Kiana told him coldly.

Ronan drew in a deep breath. He was not sure how much more of this he could take. She had been here a week and had not said much more than she had now to him.

"Okay, Kiana," Ronan hissed. "I know you don't want to hear this. But I am going to tell you anyway." He helped her onto the bed, ignoring her telling him not to.

"Please, Ronan," Kiana sighed. "I am tired. I just want to get some sleep."

"No," Ronan sat on the chair next to her bed. "You are going to hear me out."

"Fine," Kiana pulled the blanket up to her chin. "It's your house. I can't throw you out."

"Valerie and I ended months before I met you," Ronan told her. "Yes, she wanted more, but she was not the one I wanted to spend the rest of my life with. She kept sending me those messages for months after we ended it. Then her father wanted to buy up some top five-star hotels, including my uncle's, you know, the one we bumped into each other at."

"Your uncle owns the hotel?" Kiana looked at him, her cheeks starting to go red.

"Yes," Ronan nodded. "He will not sell it, so your job is safe." He shocked her by saying. "I was with my uncle when Simon phoned to have words with him about my assistant, nearly killing his assistant manager."

Kiana looked down at her hands, nodding, before blurting out the lies she had told him.

"I lied, too," Ronan looked up at her. "I broke off with Valerie the day I met you at the gym."

Kiana frowned at him.

"I also never got your number from Hayden," Ronan told

her with a small laugh. "I stole it off his phone when I put a security app on it."

"Ah," Kiana looked at him. "That is not a stalker move at all." She laughed.

They fell silent for a minute.

"Thank you, Ronan, for looking after me," Kiana told him. She was glad they had cleared the air. Kiana smiled at him. "I am glad you know the truth now," Kiana swallowed. She was not ready to tell him anymore. "I think I am going to have a little nap." She smiled.

"Of course," Ronan stood. "I have to go to work for a few hours but will be back in time for supper." He smiled and left the room.

CHAPTER 20
All That Ends Well

Kiana was going to miss her walks on the beach. During this past month of recovery, she had become used to walking by the ocean at least three times a day. But her ribs were healed, and the stitches in her head had come out at least three days ago. It was time for Kiana to return to her life, although Chloe was trying to convince her otherwise.

Magda was flying back to see them for a week, and after that, Kiana would go home to visit her family for a few days. Kiana was also going to secretly miss Ronan. They had become close but as friends over the past month. He walked with her on the beach in the morning before he went to work and then in the evening when he got home.

After dinner, they would sit and talk about anything and everything for hours. What they did not speak about and skirted around the subject was how they felt about each other. Kiana knew she was still head over heels in love with Ronan. But it was not only her she had to think about. Honestly, she also had a problem trusting in another relationship.

Kiana had decided to tell Ronan about the baby when she

was ready, which was not soon. But she already felt the strain on her clothes from the weight she was gaining. It would not be long before there was a definite change to her body shape.

Kiana stood looking out at the ocean. She was going to miss this view.

"There you are," Chloe's voice made her turn around.

"Yes," Kiana smiled. "I was saying goodbye to the ocean."

"Kiana, you have to tell Ronan how you feel," Chloe looked at her sadly.

"I see you got your ring made smaller," Kiana changed the subject.

"Yes," Chloe's eyes lit up. "I finally got it back."

"I am so happy for you, Chloe," Kiana grinned.

"And I want to be happy for you," Chloe said, linking her arm through Kiana's as they returned to the house.

"Kiana," Ronan rushed through the front door, looking frantic. "Oh, thank goodness you are still here."

"What's wrong?" Kiana looked at Ronan worriedly.

"I was so worried I had missed you," Ronan walked up to her. "Please, Kiana, don't go."

"I ..." Kiana looked into his eyes and knew she was lost.

"I love you, Kiana," Ronan suddenly dropped onto one knee and pulled out a little black velvet box. "Will you marry me?"

"Ronan," Kiana looked down at him. She knew she had to tell him now. "I'm pregnant," she blurted, "and it is your baby."

Ronan looked at her, shocked for a moment before a huge smile split his face. He stood up and pulled her to him, laughing.

"We're having a baby?" Ronan looked like a child on Christmas morning. "May I?" He asked, reaching for her tummy.

Kiana swallowed, her eyes misting over with tears as she

nodded. Ronan stepped up to her and gently cupped her rounded belly.

"Hello in there," Ronan whispered to her stomach before raising his head and grinning at her. Dropping to his knee again, "Kiana, will you marry me and let me be the father I know I can be?"

"Yes," Kiana laughed, tears spilling down her cheeks as Ronan pulled her into his arms.

Ready for more happily ever after? You'll love this small town romance. All bets are off when casino mogul Kase Chapman returns home for the pastor's daughter, Anaya McCray! The Billionaire's Bet is book 3 of the Can't Buy a Billionaire Series.

Start reading now!

Enjoy the preview!

CHAPTER 1
Time to Slow Down

Kase Chapman was a dashing, handsome young man. He owned several reputable multi-casinos throughout the States. At age thirty-two, he had already acquired eight different casinos and resorts across different states in the US. He was known as the casino owner and had the best turnaround in the industry.

Most of his peers held him in high regard for his no-nonsense approach to business and his commitment to a professional work ethic, but he didn't look like a billionaire.

When Kase was informed of what was happening right under his nose at the Silver Palms Salt Lake Casino, he felt as though someone had thrown him in the ring for a ten-round bout with Mike Tyson—with no prior training or warning.

He was known to be hard on his staff when it came to discipline and sticking to the rules when it came to gambling codes. He'd worked relentlessly for the last decade, pouring his blood, sweat, and tears into building each of his resorts. Whenever he acquired a new location, he made it his top priority to ensure things ran smoothly. This was his business method.

He'd just been thrown a curveball of epic proportions. He discovered that Austin Craig, head of operations at his Silver Palms Salt Lake Casino, had been discreetly embezzling funds. Nobody knew how long this had been going on. It was flagged during a random audit that Kase used to order for each of his casinos whenever he felt like it. It was his way of keeping everyone on their toes.

The massive casino was bustling with its bright lights and slot machines, spitting out coins intermittently. It was packed, as usual. In the back office, not even the walls of the supposed sound-proofed conference room could contain the rage in Kase's voice as he was firing off one question after another.

"I need you to tell me exactly how long this has been going on, Austin, and what sort of figures am I looking at here?" he shouted. "Has this been a one-off incident, or have you been skimming off the top for a while? Dammit, you need to answer me, or you're going to find yourself facing all the various authorities on this one." It looked as though one of the veins in his temples was about to burst. It was pulsating so rapidly.

Austin had been managing operations in Salt Lake for a little over five years. This was the first time Kase had been informed of embezzlement in the casino. His casino! Kase had been monitoring the numbers for Salt Lake for a while now. It had been all over the place, rather than functioning like the well-oiled machines of his other casinos. Could this be the reason why? He was pleased he had the foresight to go with his gut instinct in ordering that the random audit be done. He was totally devastated by the results of the audit. It's never pleasant to hear that you're being betrayed by someone you implicitly trusted.

This wasn't Kase's first rodeo, and he'd had to deal with

theft before, especially while the resorts were in the transition phase between being acquired. He personally trained key personnel on how he wanted things to run. He never had to deal with any of his general managers stealing from him, though, and it hurt like hell.

"Austin, I trusted you with running everything operationally, and I am feeling totally betrayed at this point. All that I need to know is whether there were any other staff members involved, and give me a number—even if it's an approximate one." He was beginning to calm down but remained frustrated by the tight-lipped nature of someone he'd considered a loyal employee and friend.

The silence in the conference room became deafening, and Kase eventually hammered the final nail into Austin's coffin.

"You've left me no choice other than to get the Salt Lake Police Department involved, the FBI, and the Gaming Commission. You know they'll have your license for this, and you'll never work in another casino again. I'm really sorry it had to come to this." The only response Kase received was a very solemn grimace as Austin stared down at the plush burgundy and gold carpeting that ran throughout the casino.

The silence was broken by Kase's phone's ringtone. The caller ID showed "VICKY".

"Oh shit, here we go again! I'm going to have to bail on this woman for the second time in just as many weeks."

"Hey, Vicky, yeah... I'm sorry to have to do this to you again, but I'm still in Salt Lake at the moment and have no clue what time I'll be back in Vegas, or even if I will make it back to Vegas this evening." Kase and Vicky had only been on two dates before this. Although the youthful, charming croupier from Silver Sands Vegas was interested in pursuing a serious relationship with Kase, the feelings definitely weren't mutual.

It was something Kase knew he would never be able to

commit to. His heart belonged to a girl back home, someone who had hurt him badly but nonetheless was indeed the only love of his life. Anaya.

Just the thought of her made him feel a bulge. Hopefully, nobody else is paying too much attention.

"Why, Mr. Chapman, I do think that this is the second time you've stood me up! You may just have to do something special to make it up to me." Vicky's voice was sensual, and she spoke with definite sexual overtones.

When Kase arrived back in Vegas, he'd have to explain to Vicky that things between them just weren't going to happen.

Right now, he needed to focus entirely and finish with the Salt Lake matter so he could try and tie up all the loose ends. Being responsible for more than fifty thousand permanent employees across the eight casinos was challenging. It was days like today that he wondered whether it wouldn't just be worthwhile to cash in his stakes in all the casinos and choose a quieter lifestyle somewhere. Days like this made him sick to his stomach.

He thought of retreating to his vacation home in San Diego. He'd bought it for himself on his thirtieth birthday but never got the chance to use it. What was the point of having it if he was never going to use it?

When it came to Kase's dating profile, you might say he was a bit of a player. Who wouldn't want to be seen next to the gorgeous six-foot hunk of a man? Managing multiple casinos was a daunting task. Hell, just being able to manage one of them successfully could prove challenging. However, Kase had quickly risen through the ranks of the gaming industry, taking one calculated risk after another. Fortunately for him, most of them paid off handsomely.

After a decade in the business, he became a legend within the gaming industry. However, while he was always flawlessly groomed and ready for any curveball that could be thrown at him on any of the floors of his casinos, he found this massive adrenaline rush to be his passion. It was what helped him get up in the morning and face each new day with anticipation.

There was only one ingredient missing for his life to be absolutely perfect—the girl who got away. The one who stole his heart. He had always imagined that they would be doing all of this together. While the industry thought he was a bit of a playboy, the truth was that he only dated as many women as he could as a means of trying to forget about his true love.

Boarding the Gulfstream 650ER homeward bound for Vegas, Kase poured himself a stiff double KWV on the rocks. It was sheer indulgence to drink one of the hotel's most expensive imported brandies, but what the hell? After a day like today, he needed something to take the edge off.

Running two major casinos right next to each other on the Vegas strip kept him extremely busy. Being the only resorts adjacent to each other, it made sense for him to convert one of the penthouse suites at the Silver Palms Vegas Hotel into his permanent living quarters. Vegas was like home for Kase. His reason for never getting around to San Diego was that, in a decade, Kase had hardly taken any time off. The word "vacation" was missing from his vocabulary. The only time he got out to San Diego was when he was visiting the casino nearby.

Sipping on the dark amber liquid, Kase caught himself thinking of Anaya again.

He chastised himself for thinking of her to the point where it was torturous. "She's probably married with a couple of kids running around. A beautiful girl like that isn't going to stick around waiting for me to sweep her off her feet. Besides, she broke up with me. I'm an asshole for even thinking about her," Kase would usually lament.

Pouring himself another brandy on the rocks, he settled in for the rest of the flight to Vegas, exhausted. He was pleased he'd called off his date with Vicky. He was well aware that she was after more than what he could offer her. His only reason for dating so many different women was that he didn't have to commit to any of them. No matter how many there were, none of them held a candle to the love of his life.

Arriving in Vegas, his car was already waiting for him. However, it wasn't an extremely long drive to the Silver Palms in Vegas. Vegas at night still made his heart beat faster, seeing all the lights, the people, and experiencing all the sounds from each of the casinos. This was the very lifeblood that he'd dreamed of most of his life. The only thing missing from this picture-perfect life now would have been Anaya, the woman he had so much love for.

Kase took his private elevator up to his suite and was completely overcome with fatigue. Usually, he would do the rounds at the different tables, stop in and greet all the staff, and possibly even have a drink in one of the theaters. For some reason, the events of the day had left him physically and mentally depleted. Unable to keep his eyes open, he didn't even bother getting undressed when he entered his room. After managing to take off his shoes and unbutton his shirt, he was fast asleep within minutes of his head hitting the pillow.

At 5:00 a.m., Kase was up and ready to hit the private gym. His personal trainer, Daniel, was waiting for him. Daniel noticed that Kase wasn't looking like his usual upbeat self.

"You okay today, Kase? You don't look like you're with us this morning yet," Daniel asked.

"I'm wonderful," Kase lied. The truth was that he could feel his heart pounding in his chest a lot faster than it should be at a resting position.

After warming up, he headed to the treadmill to start his cardio workout. Then he moved on to the stepper machine with the intent to push himself even harder than he did on the treadmill. It felt like he had slight indigestion. He chalked this up to not eating correctly and ignored the pain. Beginning his reps on the stepper, alternating with skipping, he'd no sooner started with his second set of skipping reps when the entire room suddenly went dark and everything around him felt surreal.

Fortunately, Daniel was within arms' reach. He stopped Kase from taking what could have been a nasty nosedive into some heavy gym equipment. Out cold, it took Daniel a few minutes to revive Kase. In the meantime, the receptionist made an emergency call to Dr. Ethan Stone, the primary on-site medical doctor for the Silver Palms Vegas and Silver Sands Vegas.

"I'm fine, really, Daniel. There's no need to fuss over anything. I was lightheaded because I didn't have dinner last night or breakfast this morning." Kase insisted there was nothing to worry about. He asked for some water and tried to stand up. Daniel insisted that he remain exactly where he was until after Dr. Stone had examined him.

"Daniel, I'm perfectly capable of walking myself to Ethan's consulting room and actually seeing him there. I'd like to hop in the shower before then, in any event." Kase usually sounded a lot more assertive and sure of himself, which made Daniel even more concerned about the overall health of the hotelier. After several unsuccessful attempts to get up on his own, Kase eventually agreed to remain where he was until Dr. Stone managed to see him. Sure enough, 15 minutes later, Ethan Stone walked in.

Taking one look at Kase, Dr. Stone would have been able to give him a reasonable diagnosis without even examining him properly. He had never seen Kase looking completely drained. There were only a few people who had watched Kase rise through the hospitality and gaming ranks as quickly as he had, and Ethan Stone was one of them.

Personally, Kase hated doctors because they reminded him of home. He was pleased that Ethan had arranged to examine him personally instead of sending one of his junior interns.

"Thanks, Ethan. What's up, Doc? Indigestion or heartburn?" Kase managed to joke, as he could now sit up with assistance. His head was still spinning, and the pounding in his chest had subsided slightly. But each of the symptoms was still there.

Nobody could fault Kase for his level of fitness. For his age, his six-foot frame was muscular and well-defined. He had to be if he was going to be successful and on top of his game in the hotel industry. He needed to be ready at the drop of a hat to be called to any of the casinos he owned.

The look on his face said it all. Clearly, Kase wasn't expecting the answer he received from Dr. Stone. One of his oldest and dearest friends was advising him to take a month's vacation where he could get away from anything and everything casino-related. Warning Kase that his situation was serious, Dr. Stone said he needed to unplug from all communications for at least a month.

"For a month? You have got to be kidding me. Do you realize that part of the time I'm going to be away is right at the beginning of the summer holidays? You know how crazy things get around here. Wouldn't it be better to wait until after the summer break when things quieted down substantially?"

"Kase, I don't think you quite understand how dangerous this is. I'm actually afraid for you right now! If you value your life, you will take what I'm telling you seriously. The next time you collapse, you may not have people around to help you. You're actually playing with your life right now. I know you think I'm just some fuddy-duddy out-of-touch doctor, but you know I don't mince my words, so here's the straight-up, no-bullshit version for you! If you don't go and get some rest, you spend a long time recovering. Your ticker isn't sounding good right now, and if you're telling me that you started with these chest pains before you walked in here this morning—well, you're just lucky you happened to be right here."

The longer Dr. Stone talked, the more ominous the diagnosis. Although Kase had initially recoiled at the idea, he was beginning to identify the uneasiness in Ethan's voice as well as the concern all over his face.

Where would he go? He only had his penthouse suite at the hotel as well as his holiday home in San Diego. By the sounds of things, he needed to be around a support system that wasn't going to add to his stress levels. San Diego was out; there were just too many staff there with prying eyes and there was no way he wanted any of them playing nursemaid to him.

There was only one other remote place where he would be able to get peace and quiet, which was his hometown. Just the thought of returning to his childhood home was enough to elevate his blood pressure even further. Was it the thought of returning home after so long, or was it because of Anaya?

What do you even pack for a month away in the middle of nowhere?

About the Author

Rose M. Cooper read her first novel when she was eight years old. Since then, she has read tens of novels and twice as many short stories. She, however, did not discover her special knack for writing romance fiction until a decade later.

Now a full-time author with a specialty in contemporary romance, Cooper writes sensual yet relatable love stories designed to hook her readers at first glance. She views writing as another outlet to creativity, and thus has no intentions of setting down her pen just yet. There are many intriguing love stories to be told, and Cooper is set to tell them all.

She hails from New York and currently makes her home in Copiague, New York with her husband, her black cat and her Maine Coon cat. When she is not writing, you will most certainly find her around computers or getting her nose stuck in a book.

facebook.com/RoseMaeCooper

twitter.com/rosemaecooper

instagram.com/rosemaecooper

tiktok.com/@rosemaecooper

amazon.com/author/rosemaecooper

WANT TO BE FIRST TO KNOW?!

JOIN MY NEWSLETTER!
ROSEMAECOOPER.COM/NEWSLETTER

Support Me By Leaving A Review!

rosemaecooper.com/One_Night_book